Books By Ruth M. Arthur

After Candlemas
The Autumn People
The Little Dark Thorn
The Saracen Lamp
The Whistling Boy
Portrait of Margarita
Requiem for a Princess
A Candle in Her Room
My Daughter, Nicola
Dragon Summer

AFTER
CANDLEMAS

AFTER CANDLEMAS

Ruth M. Arthur

ILLUSTRATIONS BY MARGERY GILL

Atheneum
1974 New York

For Connie
with love.

Copyright © 1974 by Ruth M. Arthur
All rights reserved
Library of Congress catalog card number 73–84820
ISBN 0–689–30129–4
Published simultaneously in Canada by
McClelland & Stewart, Ltd.
Manufactured in the United States of America
by H. Wolff, New York
First Edition

AFTER CANDLEMAS

Chapter One

It was early spring when it all happened, February to be exact, after Candlemas.

We ought to have been at school of course—boarding school, enduring the rigors and miseries of the chilly Easter term, but our headmistress, a nervous type, got cold feet and sent us all home soon after term started. A series of mysterious explosions had occurred in the boiler room and kitchen quarters after the conversion to North Sea gas, which was done during the Christmas holidays. And when electrical power cuts as a result of the coal shortage became more frequent and drastic, she decided to close the school for a couple of weeks.

I should explain that the school does stand in a particularly exposed area of the east coast, where the winds off the Siberian snows have full shriveling power, so I expect Miss Minnitt was right, and *we* certainly made no complaint.

The four of us in our dormitory had decided that it was too cold to undress for bed and were struggling to get our pajamas on over our under clothing when Nancy Mariner, who was in charge of our room, came prancing in with the good news.

"We're all being sent home," she cried delightedly, "tomorrow, while the repairs are done and until there's some hope of heating this barracks of a place."

"How super!" cried the other two, Patsy and Sheila, and seizing my hands they whirled me into a sort of war dance of ecstacy, till we flopped exhausted onto our beds.

Suddenly the same thought struck them, and they spoke together. "Harriet—where will *you* go?" they asked.

My parents and younger brother and sister were in Hong Kong where my father is in banking, and since I had just been out there for the three weeks of the Christmas holidays, I knew that I could not go back again so soon.

There was a short silence, and I suppose I looked a bit woebegone.

"Have you no aunts or uncles or cousins or anybody?" Patsy asked kindly. "Where do you usually go for holidays?"

4

"Most of my father's relatives live abroad. I only see them when they come home on leave, and my mother has no brothers or sisters, only the two old aunts who brought her up—I suppose I could go to them again," I said drearily.

"You can come home with me if you like, we've plenty of room." Nancy Mariner came across the room as she spoke and sat down beside me. "Would you like to do that?" she asked. "My home is in Dorset, close to the sea. My mother paints so our life is a bit haphazard, if you know what I mean."

I did not quite know what to say, and I felt myself blushing with shyness and delight.

Nancy was rather a special person, everyone liked and admired her. She was good at absolutely everything and was a year or so older than Patsy, Sheila and I. I was a little in awe of her and doubted whether I could live up to her, hence my hesitation.

"Well," she said, "what about it?"

"It's really very kind of you," I began, "but won't it be an awful bore for you, I mean, I'm lower down in the school than you are, and——"

"I can't see how that matters," said Nancy laughing, "you can do all the chores at home that I hate doing! I think you'd better come."

Her warmth and directness settled my qualms. "Thank you, Nancy, I'd love to, if you're sure I won't be a nuisance," I said.

"Don't worry, I'll see that you're not. Well that's settled, I'll go and tell the Minnitt and save her one more headache," she said.

The moment Nancy had left the room the others

turned to me. "You lucky, *lucky* clot," they chorused, "invited to stay with Nancy in her own home—some people have all the luck! You must tell us about *everything* when we all get back here again."

I grinned amiably and swore to myself to do nothing of the sort.

We were all up early next morning, shivering in the icy air, but too full of excitement to grumble much. There was a wonderful holiday atmosphere, spirits were high at the unexpected bonus, and everyone was jubilant except the few for whom school was an escape from an unhappy home.

Packing was done in next to no time, satchels crammed with books for the work at home that had been allotted to us by each member of the staff and after a noisy breakfast, good-byes were said and we were off.

The first part of the journey was all right, the train was full of chattering girls all bound for London, but when I found myself alone with Nancy on our way to Dorset I became shy and tongue-tied and began to worry that her family might not like me.

I need not have been anxious, for when we got out of the train at last, there was no one at the little station to meet us, and when after Nancy had made a telephone call and we had had a cup of tea in the porter's firelit room, Mrs. Mariner turned up full of apologies, all my fears melted away. She was a simply delightful person and I took to her at once.

"I suppose you forgot, Mum," said Nancy without rancor as they hugged one another warmly. "Well— actually I did, darlings," Mrs. Mariner acknowledged in a tone that implied such a thing surprised even herself.

"I can't think what came over me—it's gorgeous to have you both—now where on earth have I put the car keys?" she cried, patting each of her pockets in turn.

"Oh Mum! You've left them in the car, of course," said Nancy laughing, her voice full of love, "you always do—come on, Harriet!"

We climbed into the car, a scarred and muddy Land Rover, and we all squashed together in the front.

"Better stop for petrol in the village," Nancy suggested, "it's getting a bit low isn't it?"

"I *knew* there was something else I had to do," said Mrs. Mariner. "You're so good at remembering things, darling, I don't know how I ever get along without you."

We filled up the tank at the first garage and ground our way up the hill.

"How's everyone?" asked Nancy. "Michael? Pop?" (Michael is her brother) "Are you having bad power cuts?"

"Not too bad, calor gas cooking and wood fires have their good points you know, and candles give a very soft and secret light—firelight and candles conducive to confidences," Mrs. Mariner said laughing. "Everyone is O.K.," she continued. "Michael is finding it bitterly cold in Cambridge, working without heating most of the time in those high college rooms. Your father is as busy as ever, full of new schemes for making the quarries pay."

They chatted on, family talk, and after a minute or so I stopped listening and concentrated on the country we were passing through.

I had never been in Dorset before, and on this dusky January evening my first impressions were of sweeping downs and crouching valleys, of villages of stone cottages clustering round their churches, of prosperous farmhouses protected by skeleton trees. The little roads twisted steeply through the woods on the sides of the downs, up over the crests and down again to the valley on the other side.

Lights had begun to twinkle from cottage windows as we climbed a long hill and panted along the ridge. In the fields by the road huge slabs and hunks and piles of stone loomed out of the dusk, and I noticed they were scattered or grouped around great holes in the earth.

"There are my father's stone quarries," cried Nancy, pointing excitedly, "and down beyond them on that side is the sea, and there between the quarries and the sea is our house."

We turned onto a little rough lane, leaving the village behind us, ran downhill a short distance, and drew up in front of a house.

"We're home!" cried Nancy enraptured. "We're home."

Chapter Two

It was a long low house built of stone, three cottages made into one dwelling. Its back was to the ridge of the downs, the quarries and the village, and it faced south across a tangle of garden to the sea. It was simply called "Mariners" since the family had lived there for several centuries—that much Nancy had already told me, but I felt there was more, much more to learn about the house. Stonemasons by trade for generations, the Mariners, Nancy's father and his brothers now owned the inland quarries round the village.

As we burst into the house and turned on the lights, a regal white cat with great amber eyes came to inspect us, and recognizing Nancy, began to rub its side against her leg.

"Nobody at home except the Dowager," Nancy remarked cuffing the cat affectionately. She dumped her case and odds and ends on the floor.

"Leave your gear here and come and get warm, Harriet," she invited, leading the way into the sitting room.

A banked-up fire glowed on the stone hearth, and Nancy gave it a couple of digs with the poker and threw on some logs.

"There are the bellows, give it a few puffs while I put the kettle on, and we'll make some toast for tea," she said. "I'm ravenous, aren't you?"

By the time Mrs. Mariner came in from putting the car away, the tea was made and Nancy and I were busy with toasting forks before a promising blaze.

The curtains were drawn against the darkness outside and Nancy put on a record, then we settled down, the three of us and the Dowager, to tea and hot buttered toast. It was wonderfully cozy and intimate and reminded me of winter teas at home before my parents went abroad to live. How I missed my family!

Afterward Nancy took me up to my room, next door to hers, and Mrs. Mariner brought in a little jug of early snowdrops, which she set on the dressing table.

I unpacked my belongings and put them away in cupboard and drawer, then I opened the window and hung out of it snuffing the keen air. It was very quiet; only the slap and suck of the sea came up to me from the beach below the house, there was no other sound, no seabird's cry broke the silence.

When I went downstairs, the sound of laughter and cheerful voices drew me to the kitchen.

Nancy was sitting on the kitchen table, while Mrs. Mariner was chopping carrots and a dark comfortable-looking woman was peeling potatoes by the sink.

"This is Mrs. Pyke, my friend Harriet," said Nancy by way of introduction.

"Mrs. Pyke has brought us along a hare for tomorrow's dinner," Mrs. Mariner explained, "and now she won't go home till she has done some extra work."

"Might as well lend a hand while I'm here," said Mrs. Pyke laughing.

"What can *I* do?" I asked.

"Open that can of pineapple if you like," said Nancy, "while I beat up the cream. Go on, Mrs. Pyke," she continued, "you were telling us about Gramma's talk to the Women's Institute."

"She were first rate," said Mrs. Pyke proudly, "spoke for near an hour, she did, interesting too, she reads a lot and knows how to use words, all about the old days in the village it were."

"Gramma Cobbley is our local celebrity," Mrs. Mariner explained, "she's the oldest inhabitant of the village and at eighty-eight years old she misses nothing—sharp as a needle. Mrs. Pyke, who comes to help us in the house is her daughter-in-law and lives in the next cottage."

"You must meet Gramma," Nancy said to me. "Shall we come up to see her tomorrow, Mrs. Pyke?"

"Of course, you'll be very welcome anywhen," answered Mrs. Pyke. "I'd best be gettin' home now, but I'll tell Gramma on my way past to expect you and your friend tomorrow. Good night now, good night all."

As she hurried out of the back door, Mr. Mariner strode in through the front, a square solid man with a merry twinkle in his eye.

Nancy jumped up and ran and threw her arms round his neck. "Hello, Pop," she cried. "Lovely to see you!" Then remembering me, "Harriet this is my father," she said proudly.

Mr. Mariner held out his hand and drew me to him so that he stood with an arm round each of us.

"I'm very glad to see you, Harriet," he said, "any friend of Nancy's is welcome here. Your people are abroad are they?"

"Yes, in Hong Kong. I was out there for Christmas," I told him.

"Never been out of England myself," he said, "our roots are deep in Dorset, and my work is here in the quarries like my father and my grandfather and his father before him. It must be hard for you to have your family so far way. Are you the eldest?"

"Yes, I have a little brother and sister who'll be coming home to school later on," I explained. "You see it's only a year since they all went out there, and I miss them terribly. My mother's two old aunts live in Derbyshire and I went to them for the summer holidays, but it's hardly home to me. That's why it's so super of Nancy to bring me here, it's being in a real family again and I love it."

"Watch it!" warned Nancy, "he'll have you cleaning his boots before you know where you are just to make you feel you're one of us! Come on, let's help to get supper."

We went to where Mrs. Mariner was standing over the stove stirring a sauce that smelled delicious.

"Nearly ready," she said drawing the pan to the side of the flame. "Nancy, will you and Harriet set the table. I'll be back in a minute."

Nancy chuckled. "*Ten* minutes," she muttered. "She's gone to have a sherry with Dad. I doubt if I can wait that long, let's have a bite to keep us going." She pulled the crusty side off a loaf, spread it with butter and jam and cutting it in half held a piece out to me. I seized joyfully on my share and bit into it. I was just as hungry as she was.

Later, when we had finished supper, Mr. Mariner tied a striped apron round himself and started to wash the dishes, and Nancy and I dried while Mrs. Mariner made the coffee.

"There's a Western," said Nancy scanning the TV programs in the newspaper. "Anyone want to watch?"

"Of course," cried Mr. Mariner. "I never miss a Western if I can help it. Harriet? Coming to watch?"

"All right," I agreed.

"I might as well too," said Nancy, "until I fall asleep," and we all went into the sitting room with our coffee except Mrs. Mariner who said she had some telephoning to do and didn't like Westerns anyway.

Long before the film was over, I found my attention wandering as I struggled against an overwhelming sleepiness. I felt relaxed and happy and already so much one of the family that I couldn't believe I had only been in the house for a few hours. Later, when Mrs. Mariner came in with a tray of bedtime drinks, Nancy gave a huge yawn and we decided it was impossible for either of us to stay awake any longer. So we left Mr. Mariner to his pipe and his Western and Mrs. Mariner to her embroidery and dragged ourselves up the stairs to bed.

"Good night Harriet, sleep well," said Nancy from the door of my room. "Bang on the wall if you want me."

"Thanks," I said. "Good night. It's lovely to be here."

I was too sleepy to bother with a bath, and when I was ready for bed I drew back the curtains and opened the windows and stood there for a moment listening—an owl screeched near at hand, and I heard the light bark of a fox, then nothing but the sighing of the sea.

Chapter Three

There followed a spell of such mild weather that it could have been April. Sunshine streamed down from a serene blue sky, the sea lapped gently on the rocks below the house.

I couldn't wait to get on to the beach that first morning, and as soon as breakfast was finished Nancy and I ran down the path from the house to the steep cove at the bottom. The beach was unexpected, no sand but huge slabs and shelves of rock over which the waves washed leaving a great paved area as the tide receded.

We explored around in the rock pools for a bit, poking the fringed sea anemones, but found nothing more exciting than a crab or two. After a while we sat down in the sun, our backs against the sheltering cliff, and it was then that I noticed the memorial slab cut in the face of the rock behind me. "In memory of Ambrose Briddle aged 17 years drowned here on Feb. 2nd 1890. After Candlemas."

I read it again, for the wording was unusual and my curiosity was roused. Why "after Candlemas" I wondered?

"What about this?" I asked Nancy, pointing to the slab, "there's something strange here, some mystery isn't there? What exactly is Candlemas?"

"I'm not sure," Nancy confessed, "but I think it is one of the festivals of the Church. It's also got something to do with the pagan rites of spring. We could ask Gramma, she has information about all kinds of things. You could ask her about the boy too, people say he still walks the beach at times—but I don't believe in ghosts. Come on, let's have a look at the old quarries in the cliff behind us."

She jumped up and started climbing the path out of the cove. Just near the top I noticed a kind of tumbled-down shelter built of stone standing on a grassy platform. Its roof had given way and it was overgrown with nettles and brambles. I had not seen it on the way down. I stopped to have a look at it, and Nancy said, "It's an old chapel, I believe, a hermit is supposed to have lived there once."

I would have liked to stop and poke about a bit, but Nancy was keen to show me more and had already stepped up out of the cove onto the grassy ledge behind it.

I would have to come back again on my own sometime to explore more thoroughly.

I followed her to the path that led along the edge of the cliff, behind and above the place we had been sitting, a higher shelf in the rock as it were. Soon the ledge widened, and to the landward side of it were great square hollows and caves cut in the rock of the cliff. "Those are the old stone quarries," Nancy explained. "The stone used to be shipped away from here to other parts of England. They're not in use anymore, of course, not the quarries on the seacoast, only those inland round the village."

I gazed in awe at them, great square-cut holes rough-hewn and rugged, wide open to the wind, with the sea crashing and sucking below them, and behind them smaller darker caves that seemed to have been tunneled far back into the hillside toward the village, perhaps even undermining it in places. Their ceilings were jagged with wicked splinters of stone ready to fall, their floors where the sun never penetrated, damp and chilling. I shivered in the warm sunshine, what a wild desolate place, sinister too, yet it had an austere beauty, a grandeur and a glory of its own. We sat down at the mouth of one of the caves, and the crying of the gulls on the cliffs below seemed to find an echo in the rock tunnel behind us. It was eerie and strange and frightening to me, although Nancy seemed unmoved—I expect she was used to it.

"Let's go up to the village and visit Gramma," she suggested. "I think we can find a cup of coffee at home on the way past. Are you hungry?"

"Always," I confessed with a giggle.

Nancy started off, pressing ahead, but I paused to cast

lingering glances back at the cliff caves and the ruined chapel and the cove with its memorial to the boy who had died—"After Candlemas." The thought of him lingered on in my mind with surprising poignancy long after we left the beach.

We swallowed a cup of coffee and snatched a couple of buns at the Mariners' house and then went on up to the village.

It was quite small, built round a little green, a church, a school, one shop and a pub. The cottages, some roofed with stone slabs in the old way, some with thatch, were among the loveliest I have ever seen, and their names appealed to me,—"Crab Cottage," "Dimity Cottage," "Juniper Cottage," "Honeypot Cottage"—each enclosed in its own tiny garden, which in spring and summer must surely blossom in a riot of color, enchanting against the background of gray stone.

Rooks were busy at the tops of the only trees of any height, which were gathered around the church. "It's good luck to live within sound of their cawing," said Nancy.

At one end of the village, nearest to Mariners, the last cottage stood by itself, a little apart from the rest—"Ash Cottage" it was called although I didn't see any ash trees. There were a couple of beehives in the garden, and two geese with outstretched necks ran squawking at us as far as the wire netting which surrounded the orchard would allow them to.

"This is it, this is Gramma Cobbley's house," whispered Nancy, and even as she spoke, as if to investigate the cause of the commotion among the geese, a spare nimble old woman appeared in the doorway. She wore a round homemade cap of fur, which looked like a wea-sel, on top of a knitted cap that looked like a balaclava, an old-fashioned tweed jacket nipped in at the waist; a blue cotton apron covered her long skirt, and on her feet were a pair of sandshoes once white.

"Who's there?" she asked, peering at us as if she could not see very well.

"It's Nancy—Nancy Mariner. Hello, Gramma, I've brought my friend Harriet to see you." Nancy spoke slowly and clearly so that the old lady could not fail to hear her.

"Come in, come in the two of ye," said Gramma de-lightedly. "Kettle's on the boil, we'll have a cup o' tea, but wot's to do that ye be hwome from school?"

Nancy explained what had happened, and Gramma cackled with laughter.

"Wot's the use in goin' to boardy school?" she cried. "They has to send ye hwome if anything goes wrong. Well 'tis nice that ye be here anyway."

We sat in her little kitchen drinking our tea and the inquisitive geese looked in at us through the window.

"We've been down on the beach," Nancy told her. "Harriet has never been here before, our coast and the old sea quarries are all quite new to her . . ."

"And the ruined chapel and the memorial tablet to the boy who was drowned, after Candlemas," I broke in. "I think Dorset is a most exciting place—different, dis-tinctive—what I've seen of it so far."

Gramma took her wire-rimmed spectacles from an empty flowerpot on the table, put them on and leaning toward me she gave me a long and searching look, as if she were summing me up.

"Oh yes," she said nodding her head, "Dorset be all right for them that belongs *inside*, though zome o' them has memories too long for my liking."

I wondered whatever she meant? She seemed to be saying something profound but I could not grasp her meaning. There was bitterness in her voice and something else I could not quite place—the thought crossed my mind that she would make a formidable enemy.

She sat staring out of the window, lost to us as if her mind had wandered away into some private world—Nancy's question recalled her. "When is Candlemas?" she asked.

"February second, Thursday next," replied Gramma promptly.

"Oh, and what happens then?" Nancy continued. Gramma looked startled, almost affronted.

"Never you mind," she snapped, then softening her tone she added, "take a wold 'ooman's advice and bide indoors on that day after zun-down—both of ye. It b'aint safe to be about then."

Chapter Four

We stayed for some time with Gramma, who soon became friendly again and was obviously enjoying our company, and before we left her we had promised to come again soon.

We had brought quite a lot of schoolwork with us and knew we ought to get on with some that afternoon, but we decided it was a waste not to be out while the mild weather lasted.

After lunch when we had done the washing up we left Mrs. Mariner to her painting, each took an apple in our pockets and went off together to walk along the cliffs to the next cove.

We didn't meet a soul all the way as we followed the path up then down the steep grassy slope of one headland after another. There was little wind in the clear sky, and the deep blue swell of the sea rolled unbroken. Far out on the horizon the occasional outline of a ship showed for a few minutes and was gone, or the faint chug of a fishing boat engine came up to us from near in shore where they were settting the lobster pots.

When we were tired, we lay in the sun on the tough dry grass and munched our apples in silence and contentment. It was easy to imagine that it was April until too early the sun began to sink, ending the short January day, and we turned for home.

Nancy seemed to flag a bit on the way back, and we had several stops for rests.

"Are you all right?" I asked noticing her pallor.

"Only rather tired," she said, "and my throat hurts. Perhaps I'm starting a cold."

But we forgot about it when we got in for tea beside the log fire, and while we toasted crumpets on long forks and ate them sloshy with butter, Mrs. Mariner asked me about Hong Kong, and I told her my impressions.

"I was only there for three weeks, my first visit, and our friends are European, I did not meet the Chinese. My father has not been there long enough to have made Chinese friends," I said.

I found myself describing the country and the busy island humming with life; the paddy fields on the mainland with their water buffalo and workers in huge hats; the orchards of peachblossom; the harbors tightly packed with little boats—the sampans where the poor fishermen lived; the beautiful and exotic shops for the wealthy foreigners; the narrow alleys crammed with tiny stalls, the dark market thronged with Chinese who carried their baskets of goods hung on a long pole slung across the shoulders—it was all there in my mind, a vivid clear-cut picture, a tableau, a painting in which I myself had no part. I was outside it all. I had never thought about it before, and suddenly I knew what Gramma had meant when she said of the village, "It's all right for them that belongs *inside*."

"You give a very lively description," said Mrs. Mariner. "It must be a fascinating place, you're lucky to have been there."

"Yes, I know," I replied, "and I'll be going again. I only had time for a quick glance over the surface. But I feel that however long I lived there I could never really *belong*, it is all too different, too alien, I could never be anything but a stranger."

"It's a feeling that can be very daunting to one's self-confidence," Mrs. Mariner said thoughtfully, "but of course you had your own family there so you were all right."

"Oh yes," I agreed, "I was lucky, I had support."

But the thought stayed in my mind, the idea of belonging was a new one to me. I had always belonged inside, it had never before come home to me that this was not true of everyone.

Nancy went early to bed with a hot lemon-and-honey drink and an aspirin, hoping to ward off her threatened cold, and I chose a book from the tightly packed bookshelves in the sitting room and soon followed her, leaving

Mr. and Mrs. Mariner cozily together on the couch watching TV.

I opened my window wide before I got into bed and then lay listening to the background rush of the sea. My thoughts turned again to the cove with its echoing quarries, its ruined chapel, to that lonely memorial stone on the beach, to the boy with the unusual name, Ambrose Briddle. I wondered what had happened to him, how he had been drowned, what kind of boy he was, whether he had belonged to the village or was a stranger from the world outside? The date on the stone was not so very long ago, perhaps Gramma would remember him? Perhaps if I asked her she would tell me the story, but I'd have to catch her in the right mood. I had already seen that she could be awkward.

The next day when I woke early in the morning before it was really light, there was a thickish mist and the foghorn was moaning. The house was still asleep and since it seemed too soon to get up, I started to write a long letter to my parents explaining what had happened at school and how Nancy had brought me to her home and how much I liked the Mariners and their house and everything about them.

"As for Dorset—it has the feel of country that goes far back in time, as if modern ways had only scratched its surface and underneath, deep and hidden, its secret life goes on in the same way it has for centuries. It has beauty and wildness and danger, and a magic all its own," I wrote.

By the time I had finished my letter and was ready to get up, there were distinct sounds of breakfast being prepared.

When I was dressed, I tapped on Nancy's door and put my head round it.

Nancy lay huddled up in bed and I thought at first she was still asleep, but she raised a tousled head and gave a sort of croak, and I saw that her face was blotchy and flushed as if she had a temperature—she looked simply awful!

"Stay where you are," I said, I'll fetch your mother."

I ran downstairs and found Mrs. Mariner in the kitchen and told her.

"I'll finish cooking breakfast," I offered, "and look after Mr. Mariner if you want to go to Nancy."

I made the toast and the coffee and dealt out two good platefuls of bacon and sausages and eggs and had just set them on the table in the kitchen when Mr. Mariner came in.

" 'Morning, me dear," he said putting his arm around my shoulders, "did you sleep comfortably? Where is everyone?"

I explained about Nancy and poured out his coffee for him.

"It's not like her to be out of sorts!" he exclaimed. "Maybe she picked up a flu germ on the train. You'd better stay away from her for a day or two, Harriet. Now, help yourself to what you want. You won't mind if I have a look at the paper?"

It was just how my own father behaved at breakfast, oblivious to his surroundings, so I didn't say a word, but tucked in to my plate of bacon and eggs.

Mrs. Mariner came down presently looking worried.

"Nancy's got a high temperature," she said, "and a very nasty looking throat. I think I'll ring Dr. Sloane at

25

once to come and see her. She says her throat is very painful indeed and she is feeling dreadful."

"Shall I look in on him on my way to work?" asked Mr. Mariner wresting his attention momentarily from his paper.

"No, no, I'll ring him now, thanks," Mrs. Mariner replied. Then turning to me, "You'd better keep out of Nancy's room," she warned me, "till after the doctor has seen her. Can you amuse yourself for a bit?"

"Oh yes, I'll get some schoolwork done," I said.

Chapter Five

The doctor said Nancy had glandular fever, and was quite ill. She'd have to spend at least a week in bed, and I was on no account to go near her.

"I'm terribly sorry, Harriet," said Mrs. Mariner, "it's going to be rather dull for you on your own, I'm afraid, would you rather go to one of your other friends?"

"Oh no, please, I'd like to stay on here if you'll let me, I'm sure there are things I could do to help," I pleaded. "Poor Nancy, it's terribly bad luck, but perhaps she'll get better sooner than we think."

"Of course we'd like you to stay," Mrs. Mariner assured me, "so long as you can find enough to do and not feel bored—and above all don't get ill yourself!"

I made myself scarce all morning, getting on with my work in my room, but as lunchtime approached I went down to the kitchen to see if I could help Mrs. Pyke by setting the table or something.

"You can put this potato soup through the blender for me," she said. "I thought that Nancy might fancy a drop of it. 'Tis a shame she's ill," she continued, "it's lonely for ye too on yer own like. Drop into my cottage any-when if ye want to, and I'm sure Gramma would be pleased to see ye too, she's always glad of a chat."

"Thanks, I will," I said, "and please tell me of any jobs I could do for Mrs. Mariner after you've gone."

"Well—there's a bit of ironin'," said Mrs. Pyke, "and we're in the middle of marmalade makin', plenty of oranges to cut up and jars to wash—oh I'm sure Mrs. Mariner can find plenty to keep ye busy while Nancy is ill," she finished.

"Well, tomorrow is Sunday and Mr. Mariner will be at home, so I won't come to see Gramma till Monday," I said. "D'you think she'd really like to see me?"

"O' course she would," Mrs Pyke assured me. "Don't let yerself be put off by her tart little ways, she's good-hearted really, ye know, and she'll be pleased to have a visit from ye."

"I'll go then," I said, "on Monday. She's an independent old lady, living alone at her age, I admire that."

"Oh she's independent all right, and has her likes and her dislikes. Well, I'll be off—Tara for now," said Mrs. Pyke.

Sunday passed and Nancy was no better. Mrs. Mariner would not leave her so I went out in the car with Mr. Mariner and he drove me along the enchanting coast and back through the lovely villages of the inland valleys. It was Monday afternoon before I was free to go up to visit Gramma.

I walked to the village by the shortcut through the fields, stopping on the way to talk to a friendly donkey, then having roused the geese to screechings of alarm, I reached the front of Gramma's cottage.

I rapped on the door, almost dislodging the worn horseshoe which was nailed above the cracked paint. "It's Harriet," I called opening the door, "Nancy Mariner's friend. May I come in?"

I took her by surprise, she had evidently been enjoying an afternoon nap, dozing in her chair, for her cap was askew and she looked slightly startled. I apologized for disturbing her and told her that Nancy was ill.

"That's bad," she said perking up with interest, "so ye be on yer own, ye was right to come here. Zit down now and tell me about yerself."

So I told her about my family and my travels during the Christmas holidays and answered the questions she kept asking me, for Gramma was full of curiosity, even inquisitive in an unobjectionable way.

We had been talking so hard that neither of us had noticed how the sea mist had crept up unobserved, surrounding the cottage, shutting us off in an eerie silence broken only by the moaning of the foghorn. In the garden I saw a collection of Gramma's limp garments hanging on the clothesline.

"I'll fetch them in for you," I said jumping up.

"Thanks, me dear," said Gramma. I felt relieved that she was in one of her good moods and wondered whether I dare ask her about the boy Ambrose Briddle.

By the time I had draped the wet things across the line in the back kitchen, Gramma had got the kettle on for a cup of tea and had taken down her best flowery cups from the dresser shelf and set them on the kitchen table, so I knew that she was pleased with me. She produced a chocolate roll and cut it into wedges, and we sat down together companionably.

"Now," she said, "what is it ye wants to know?"

I blinked at her, startled. How could she tell? Her eyes alert and interested were concentrated on my face.

"It's all right," she said. "I know there's zomethin' on yer mind, go on, ask me."

She had paved the way for me and having gulped down half my cup of tea I took courage and blurted out, "Tell me about the boy who was drowned, after Candlemas. You must have been alive then, do you remember him?"

"I remembers the talk about it after it happened," said Gramma, "a poor vagrant boy he were, a stranger, come to find work in the quarries. He lived down in one o' them wold caves by the sea above the cove where he were drowned. They say he do haunt the shore to this day, a restless ghost. It were supposed to be an accident, but . . . well, it were Candlemas, ye see."

"What do you mean?" I asked. "What had that to do with it?"

"Everythin'," said Gramma lowering her voice, "maybe he did see wot he shouldn't have, maybe they was afeared he'd report about their goin's on."

"You can't mean that he was deliberately drowned, got rid of?" I gasped.

"That's wot my . . . wot zome folks zaid," Gramma muttered.

"But what did he see? Smuggling? D'you mean he caught them at it, people from this village?"

"Not zmugglin'," Gramma whispered, "worse than zmugglin'—witchcraft!"

"*Witchcraft?*" I repeated incredulously. "Witchcraft *here*, in this village? You mean the boy watched them and they drowned him because he saw too much?"

Gramma nodded. "That's wot they zay," she said.

A shiver ran up my spine. "You see, as I zaid," she went on, "it were Candlemas, the first of the four great witch sabbats. Candlemas marks the comin' of spring, the sowing time, the new beginnin'. They welcomes the return of light after the darkness of winter. They keeps Candlemas with all the wold customs to this very day."

"You seem to know a lot about it, Gramma," I said, impressed, "where did you learn it all?"

"Never you mind," she snapped, suddenly wary. "I has cause to know."

Chapter Six

All of a sudden the daylight began to go as the mist
crept even closer round the village.

"I'd better get back," I said rising to my feet, "thanks
for the tea and everything, Gramma. May I come again?"

"Yes, anywhen, and remember wot I told ye, keep
to the house after zun-down on Thursday."

I pulled the hood of my anorak up as I shut the door
behind me, and I noticed that the geese were huddled
together in their shed, silent for once.

I fairly hurtled down the field path then out onto the

track which led to the cove. As I ran, the moaning of the foghorn came up to me and I had the strange sensation of plunging through the dense white mist—denser than ever nearer the sea—into a strange sinister world outside my experience.

It would have been easy in those conditions to have passed by the house without even seeing it, but I was on the lookout for the gate and breathed a sigh of relief as I turned into the garden and saw a light in Nancy's room.

Mrs. Mariner met me at the door and shook the drops of moisture off my damp coat.

"I wondered where you'd got to," she said, relief in her voice. "It's almost dark."

I told her I'd been with Gramma all the afternoon.

"Filling your head with her stories no doubt. Don't take them too seriously, Harriet, she thrives on drama."

I laughed but I didn't change my opinion of the old woman, she knew all right what she was talking about.

"How's Nancy?" I asked. "Any better?"

Mrs. Mariner shook her head. "She's feeling rotten I'm afraid, I'm so sorry this had to happen. Are you sure you wouldn't rather go on to stay with someone else?"

"Oh no," I cried. "Honestly, I like being here, but do let me help you when I can." I couldn't explain to her that nothing would make me leave now, things were becoming much too interesting.

I spent the whole of the next day doing schoolwork, pages of it. I felt I wasn't missing much out of doors, for the mist still hung about and I found it depressing and was glad to stay in.

But the first of February brought an abrupt change in the weather, the mist cleared and the sun shone warmly again from a clear blue sky. My spirits rose with spectacular suddenness until I felt lighthearted and gay. I gave what help I could in the house, but after Mrs. Pyke arrived I went off down to the cove. I made at once for the nearest cave, cautiously clambered over the chunks of rock strewn inside it and crept into one of the old quarry tunnels that burrowed into the hillside.

Stupidly I had not brought a flashlight with me so my exploration was limited by the light; the tunnel into the hillside seemed to go back forever. I came to a bend and dared not go on further into the blackness ahead for it was damp and eerie and there was an overpoweringly pungent smell.

Suddenly the cave above and around me came alive with the flittering and swooping and flapping of dozens of wings—a horrible nightmare of disturbance round my head.

I ducked, wildly waving my arms to keep them off my face, my hair, then swallowing my screams, I fled with a pounding heart back the way I had come.

It was only when I reached the entrance that my panic subsided and I hit on the rational explanation—bats, dozens of bats, I had intruded into their secret den disturbing their dreams.

My knees felt weak with relief as I sat down on a rock and broke into hysterical giggling.

I waited till I felt calm again—there wasn't a soul about —then I wandered down into the cove, to have another look at the memorial stone—poor boy, poor Ambrose, I wondered what he had seen and how much truth there was in Gramma's story.

I sat for a little in the sun below the ruined chapel. It

was so tiny it was really more like a hermit's cell, but in spite of the clear light and the warm sunshine the whole cove had an eeriness that did not encourage one to linger in it. I turned my back on it and took the path up toward the village and Gramma's cottage.

The geese warned everyone of my approach with hissing and cackling and outstretched necks, but I walked boldly past them and knocked on the door.

There was no answer so I knocked again and louder, but Gramma was not there. I felt disappointed, deflated—I had been looking forward to her company, but perhaps she hadn't gone far. Perhaps if I walked up to Mr. Mariner's stone quarries behind the village she might be home again by the time I got back.

When I came to the church I hesitated for a moment, then stepped inside—early Norman I remembered Nancy telling me. It was empty and very beautiful, its serenity guarded by two medieval knights of carved stone who lay in full armor, resting on their tombs. Before the altar stood a basket—had someone left her shopping behind? I tiptoed up the aisle to look and found that the basket was half-full of candles.

"They must be for Candlemas," I said aloud. So there *was* to be a service. I might try to come to it, I thought.

I walked on then through the village, past the school and the shop to the fields along the main road to where the busy quarries were being worked. Great hunks of rock were being dug out of the deep craters in the earth by bulldozers, lifted to the surface and cut by a machine into smaller chunks. These in their turn were trimmed by hand into sizable building blocks. Everywhere there was the sound of chipping and hammering as the stonecutters worked and the grinding of gears as the heavy trucks carted the stone away to where it was needed.

"How was the stone moved in the old days before there were trucks?" I asked one man as he chipped away with hammer and chisel at a slab of stone on a trestle outside one of the sheds.

"In my gramfer's day stwone were loaded into baskets and carried on donkeys," he said laughing, "perty zlow work compared wi' now."

I asked him if Mr. Mariner was about, but the man shook his head. "He'll be along at one o' the other workin's I reckon," he said, "he's a girt one vor a-walkin' about."

After a little while I drifted away and walked back to the village, pausing once again to knock on Gramma's door, but she had not come back, the cottage was still empty.

I walked on down to Mariners feeling slightly disconsolate, at least disappointed to have missed Gramma. She was somebody to talk to, and with Nancy ill and Mrs. Mariner so busy I needed a friend.

Chapter Seven

I woke to a morning of sunshine—February second, Candlemas. I felt deliciously lazy and lay listening to a strange sound, a rushing sound, a beating and a fluttering. I thought at first it was the wind, but it wasn't, the morning was perfectly still; it was the sound of wings, wings beating the air, hosts of them. I got up and crossed the room to look out of my open window—nothing, not a bird in sight, nor a breath of wind.

As suddenly as it had come, the sound receded and died away and there was a deep silence.

37

I was mystified and stood waiting, listening for the sound to be repeated but it did not come again, even the sea was still.

As I dressed, I had a curious feeling of anticipation, as if something unusual was about to happen to me.

Yet at breakfast everything was perfectly normal, Mr. Mariner silently munching behind his paper, Mrs. Mariner sipping her coffee listlessly.

"How's Nancy today?" I asked with a longing for her company. "Can't I go in to see her yet?"

"You should wait another day or two," said Mrs. Mariner, "though she really does seem a bit better this morning. I thought I might get the second lot of marmalade made this afternoon," she remarked without enthusiasm.

"Oh yes do, and I'll help you," I said with relief. It was something practical to do, something to counteract my vague feeling of disquiet.

"I'll be going up to the village later this morning," I said, "is there anything you want?"

Mrs. Mariner shook her head absentmindedly.

"It's Candlemas," I said. "I might go to the service in the church. I suppose it will be about eleven."

"*Is* there a service?" Mrs. Mariner asked vaguely.

I told her about the basket of candles before the altar.

"Candlemas, of *course*," she said, suddenly with me again. "I remember now, old Simeon's prophecy of the infant Christ, 'a light to lighten the gentiles,' and the candle is the symbol of that light."

"Oh is that the Christian explanation? I didn't know," I said thinking of Gramma and her preoccupation with the *pagan* side of it.

I set off for the village just before eleven and went straight to the church. I pulled open the heavy door and peeped in unobserved. There was only a handful of people in the pews, elderly mostly, there were no children, and this surprised me. The scent of incense was heavy in the air, and the service was about to begin, with the Vicar's blessing the candles.

I waited only a minute before I slipped outside again, closing the door behind me. I had not enough courage to join in, as the only young person there I'd be most conspicuous.

I walked along to Gramma's cottage but when I tried the door it was locked. Gramma must have taken the bus into town or perhaps walked along to the farm to fetch her eggs.

I wandered along the road a little way and was trying to decide what to do next when a sudden waft of organ music caught my ear. I turned and walked back to the church, but this time I did not go to the front entrance but round to a little side door. I wanted to remain unseen. I opened the door a crack and the swell of the music met me lifting my heart with joy. The little group of worshipers led by the Vicar were walking round the church in solemn procession, each person holding a lighted candle. I watched the almost medieval scene for a few moments, then before anyone noticed me I closed the door and slipped away. Once back at Mariners I worked hard for the rest of the day helping Mrs. Mariner with her marmalade making. The oranges had to be boiled and sliced into strips, then stirred with sugar and water in a vast pan and boiled till the liquid set, then it was poured into pots—pounds and pounds of the golden stuff, to be covered later when it had cooled.

It was teatime when Mrs. Mariner and I, flushed and satisfied, relaxed into armchairs by the fire.

"What a relief to get it finished. Thank you *very* much for your help, Harriet dear," she said. "Now I can relax until it's time for fruit picking and jam making in the summer—domesticity bothers me, I hate it, but it's got to be done."

"I rather enjoy it," I confessed, "and here it makes me feel . . . well, that I belong, that I'm one of the family, if you see what I mean."

Mrs. Mariner put out her hand and patted my knee. "I'm very glad that you feel like that about us," she said warmly.

The sun had gone and the lingering evening light was beginning to fade into dusk—before long it would be dark. I remembered Gramma's warning to keep indoors after sundown, but it was early yet, and I longed for a breath of fresh air.

"I'm going out for a short walk before it gets dark," I told Mrs. Mariner.

"O.K. but don't be too long," she said. "I'll go up beside Nancy for a while."

I put on my sneakers, pulled a thick sweater on over my jeans, and made for the path to the cove. Down toward the beach I hurried, but instead of going right down to the edge of the sea I turned along the cliff path past the old quarries and stood looking down. The tide was out, and below me little waves kept breaking over the slabs of rock which made a kind of shelving beach, there was no sand.

40

Now and then a sea gull cried from the ledges on the cliff side where they made their nests.

I went on quickly past the cave where the bats had startled me so the previous day, and I scrambled up the steep path that led on over the headland.

There wasn't a soul in sight as I strode along the top of the cliffs for half an hour or so before I turned for home.

Stars were beginning to prick the sky when I got back to the sea quarries again, along the edge of the hill the first lights of the village had begun to twinkle.

I had reached the main path from the cove up past Mariners to the village when I hesitated, knowing that I ought to go back inside—it was after sundown although not yet really dark—but that feeling of anticipation was strong in me again, the gentle dusk seemed vibrant with enticing secrets just beyond my hearing, surely no harm could come to me if I lingered outside for a little longer...

I took one swift look at the lighted windows of Mariners to reassure myself, then I turned and plunged past the crumbling chapel down onto the beach.

I did not go to the water's edge but stood by the memorial stone peering at it, running my finger over the letters. It was too dark to read but I knew the words by heart and murmured them aloud——"In memory of Ambrose Briddle aged 17 years, drowned here on Feb. 2nd 1890. After Candlemas."

The sea gently sucking and sighing over the rocks seemed to whisper back to me "After Candlemas... after Candlemas." This very day was Candlemas, a Christian festival but also a pagan one. I had seen the service in the church, the symbolism of the lighted candles—were there other celebrations to be held tonight, I wondered, of an older darker nature?

Were there really witches in the village as Gramma had said? Who were they? Had I unwittingly brushed up against them among the harmless looking people of the village, in the shop, in the village street, at the bus stop?

I shivered, and turning my back on the beach I scrambled up out of the cove onto the path that led to Mariners and the village. Then, pausing for a moment to get my breath, I turned and looked back toward the sea . . . and froze to the stillness of stone. There, silhouetted against the last of the light stood the thin hazy figure of a boy. I saw him walk slowly across the rock at the edge of the sea, his head bent as if he were searching for something.

I gave a little gasp of alarm, and my heart began to thump very loudly. I shut my eyes, took a deep breath to steady myself, and looked again. He was still there.

Slowly he moved along the beach, his attention fixed on the rocks at his feet, while I stood as if under a spell, scared but fascinated by the intriguing notion that I was seeing my first ghost.

It *must* be him, it *must* be the ghost of the boy who was drowned after Candlemas, the day was right, and Gramma had warned us not to go out.

Suddenly it was as if her voice spoke urgently in my ear—"bide indoors after zun-down"—the last of the light had already faded into darkness.

Blind panic hit me then and sent me scuttling up the path like a frightened rabbit. I ran the whole way without daring to look back and burst into the house breathless and shaken.

"Is that you at last, Harriet?" Mrs. Mariner called from the kitchen. "Wherever have you been?"

Firelight sprang from the crackling logs on the great stone hearth of the living room, strains of Bach floated serenely down the stairs from Nancy's room soothing and calming me, giving me reassurance. I was inside once again, safe. The tension died out of me, and I relaxed.

"Yes, it's me, I answered. "I hope you weren't worried about me. I went . . . farther away than I expected to."

I wished very much that I could go and tell Nancy of my experience, could talk to someone of my own generation who wouldn't just laugh at me, someone who was as unsure of reality as I was myself. But there was no one.

"Come and taste this sauce," Mrs. Mariner called, and I shook myself, metaphorically speaking, and strode into the kitchen.

Mrs. Mariner looked up as I came in, then looked again more sharply. "Are you all right?" she asked. "You're very pale. Why did you go so far, you've exhausted yourself, you silly child. Are you really feeling O.K.? I do hope you're not sickening for Nancy's complaint."

I laughed and assured her that I was perfectly all right. "I'm sorry," I said. "I'm afraid I've worried you. Did you think I'd got lost?"

Mrs. Mariner chuckled. "Well, something like that I must admit. It's quite dark now, you see, and the path along the cliffs can be tricky. Anyway, you're safely back, don't go so far another time will you?"

I promised her I wouldn't and went upstairs to get tidy

for supper, calling out a greeting to Nancy as I passed her door. Her voice when she responded was still pretty husky, but she sounded quite cheerful. She must be on the mend.

I went and had a bath and changed into my best slacks and my only cashmere pullover—its dreamy softness subtly soothed and comforted me.

Then I opened the window and leaned out into the quiet night, and I thought of that forlorn figure on the beach. I wondered if he still lingered there, alone in the darkness, part of the vast outside, lost in the huge emptiness of time. I was filled with compassion and with pity, for the boy he once was, a boy who had come to a tragic end—well might I spare him a thought, from the security of my warm and lighted corner inside the home of my friends.

Chapter Eight

During supper the conversation turned to the house, to
Mariners, and I had a chance to ask about its history. It
was over 300 years old Mr. Mariner told me, and con-
sisted of three cottages built for stonecutters, although
the remains of older dwellings had been found on the site.

"A great place for smuggling this cove was once, with
the old sea quarries so near," said Mr. Mariner. "This
house must have been right in the thick of it. Many a
smuggling seaman, so they say, found safe hiding and a
welcome under this roof. Like homing pigeons they came

45

for shelter, for refuge, when they were hard pressed. All that was a long time ago, of course. It was my grandfather who made the three cottages into one house—and now it's mine," he said, with pride.

"And the ruined chapel in the cove?" I asked

"It's only a hermit's cell I think," said Mr. Mariner. It hasn't been used by anyone as long as I can remember."

"And the boy who was drowned in the cove, Ambrose Briddle, d'you know what happened?"

"Oh no, it was long before my day," said Mr. Mariner laughing. "He was probably mixed up with smuggling or something. I seem to remember hearing some story. But why do you want to know?"

"I'm interested, that's all. I enjoy a bit of local color," I said to justify my curiosity.

What interested me was that Mr. Mariner, who had lived in this village all his life, seemed unaware of the sinister undercurrents beneath its smiling face. Gramma now, she was quite different, her ear closer to the ground perhaps, she certainly knew what was going on, there wasn't much that she missed.

I plodded through some schoolwork in my room after our meal. It was a warm and drowsy evening, and when I had done my stint for the day, I felt so sleepy that I decided to go early to bed. I went downstairs to say good night and was persuaded to stay for a cup of tea so that it was well after ten when I went sleepily upstairs again. The old wood of the floorboards cracked as I trod on them; the house creaked and rustled as it settled itself to sleep.

I undressed and folded back my bedcover, and after a quick wash I crossed to the window and opened it wide

to the mild night. As I stood there listening, it started
. . . far off over the sea at first, but swiftly coming nearer,
the rushing sound of wings, the sound I had heard in the
early morning. Soon it sounded as if a host of birds were
circling the house, sweeping with beating wings over and
around it, till the beating became a fluttering, a settling
to rest for the night. Not one single bird could I see.

It was the strangest sensation, to hear so clearly and to
see nothing, *nothing*, but I was not in the least disturbed
or alarmed. On the contrary, I was filled with a sense of
tranquillity, a serene comfortable feeling, for I felt that
the host of unseen birds were the protectors, the guardians of the house.

As I climbed into bed I remembered what Mr. Mariner
had said about those seamen turned smuggler who came
to the house for shelter "like homing pigeons they would
come" he had said. Not pigeons surely but *seabirds*, they
came seeking refuge for the night, spirits of wandering
seamen long dead, who still returned to the house that
had given them sanctuary. It was the only explanation I
could make, but I liked it.

I couldn't have been long asleep when something disturbed me. I sat up in bed half awake, and thought I
heard the murmur of hushed voices and the sound of
furtive feet going past the house on the path down to the
cove. But who on earth would choose to be out so late
at night in such a lonely spot?

My common sense told me I must be dreaming so I
turned over and went straight off to sleep again.

When I woke it was broad daylight but a gray morning, muffled, secret.

When I shut my window and as I dressed, I kept my

ears alert listening for the sound of departing wings, but nothing happened, they must have gone before I woke.

Mr. Mariner had already left, and I apologized for being late.

"I must have overslept a little," I explained. "I think I was awake for a bit in the middle of the night."

"Did something disturb you?" asked Mrs. Mariner as she arranged Nancy's breakfast tray. "Perhaps you had too many blankets over you, this mild weather is most unusual."

"Perhaps," I replied, "but I thought I heard noises like a group of people going down to the cove."

Mrs. Mariner laughed easily. "Hardly," she said, "not at that time, you must have been dreaming. Now, help yourself to what you want while I take Nancy's breakfast up."

Nancy seemed much perkier Mrs. Mariner reported when she came down again and joined me at the table for another cup of coffee. "Perhaps the doctor will come today and we'll ask him if you can go in to see her tomorrow."

"Oh that would be lovely," I cried, for I really was missing her, somebody of my own age to chat with.

I spent the morning writing a French essay and very boring it was, but after lunch I decided to go out. The weather had brightened a bit and I wanted to have another and closer look at the old quarry caves above the cove. I told Mrs. Mariner I'd be in by teatime before it got dark, and I ran down the path to the cove humming to myself.

When I came to the ruined chapel, I was astonished to see that the grass around it had been trodden and trampled by many feet, and inside the chapel itself were the remains of a fire and one or two candle ends. I remembered then the voices in the night, and I wondered.

The beach was entirely deserted, empty, bare, there was no sign of the boy I had seen the night before, only a few sea gulls crying over the gray water added to the melancholy.

I did not go down into the cove but turned along the cliff to the old sea quarries. I carefully avoided the first cave, I did not want to encounter its bats again. But I went into the next, a shallow opening partly blocked with several huge chunks of rock which at one time had fallen from its roof. There were other jagged pieces that looked quite ready to fall too and instinctively I covered my head with my arms and beat a hasty retreat.

The next cave looked much more promising, for several smaller tunnels ran back from it into the hillside, toward the village, and there were side passages as well which I wanted to explore. Like a fool I had again forgotten to bring a flashlight with me, but it didn't matter much, I meant to come again. This was only a preliminary exploration.

I wandered about just inside the entrance examining the floor and the great cracks in the roof, noticing the ledges and crannies and the way in which the sound of the sea echoed round the walls. What a marvelous place for smugglers! How often it must have been used as a hiding place for forbidden cargoes!

I wandered in a bit farther keeping my eyes wide open so as not to miss anything of interest. Soon I reached a turning which branched off the main cave, I stepped into it peering through the gloom along a tunnel, but it was too dark to see anything. I would have to wait till I had a light.

Suddenly I had the feeling someone was there, I thought I heard a sound and I felt frightened. I turned to get out as quickly as I could. From the darkness behind me a hand shot out and clapped itself over my mouth, and an arm came round my throat pinning me back helpless against a shoulder.

I struggled to free myself but the grip was too strong for me. There was nothing much I could do. I tried to bite the hand over my mouth. I tried to scream but I had to fight for breath, the hold of the arm pressing on my neck was half strangling me. I wriggled and squirmed. I kicked backward with my feet. I tore with my hands at the arm that held me prisoner. But it was useless, the person, a man or a boy, I assumed, was too strong for me. My head began to throb as if it would burst, the pressure round my throat tightened and I started to gasp, desperately trying to get air. Then suddenly I let my knees go limp and slumped against him hoping he'd think that I had fainted. I must have alarmed him, for the pressure round my throat loosened although the hand still covered my mouth.

"Promise not to make a sound if I let go," whispered a voice in my ear. "*Promise.*"

I nodded my head since I could not speak, and as the hand was removed I slithered to my knees.

Chapter Nine

The voice that had spoken was young and nervous, and to my surprise—quite gentle. In the dim light the figure I saw standing before me was not a man but a boy, a boy not much older than myself. I thought at once of the figure I had seen on the beach, my poor ghost—could it have been *this* boy? He was certainly real enough. Ruefully I felt my bruised throat and shoulder, and taking out my handkerchief I rubbed my mouth with it.

"What on earth did you have to do that for?" I asked, angry now as well as frightened.

"Because I couldn't risk you screaming," he answered. "Nobody knows I'm here . . . and that's the way I want it," he finished roughly.

It was a sensitive voice really, although the violence he had shown me seemed to deny it. I began to calm down, finding to my surprise that once I was free I was more intrigued by him than intimidated. Besides I could see that his hands were shaking.

"What are you doing here?" I asked. "You gave me an awful fright! Are you camping or something?"

"Not exactly," he replied. "I'm . . . well . . . I'm hiding."

"*Hiding?*" I repeated puzzled. "Who from?"

"It's a long story," the boy put tensely. "You wouldn't understand."

"How do you know till you try me?" I retorted.

He let that pass and we went on staring at one another through the gloom of the cave.

"What's your name?" I asked.

"Birney."

"Birney what?"

"Just Birney," he said sharply. "What's yours?"

"Harriet. I'm staying with friends here at Mariners."

I began to feel chilly, the cave was damp, and my throat ached where he'd squeezed it. I tried massaging it.

"Did I hurt you?" he asked.

"Yes," I told him bluntly.

He didn't apologize and I began to feel angry again.

"I think I'll go now," I said getting up.

"I don't think so," he flashed, seizing my arm. "You'll tell people about me. I've got to stop you."

I had a moment of panic, how did he mean to *stop* me?

"Why should I want to tell anyone about you?" I asked. "Who are you afraid of—the police? Have you done something awful?"

"Yes," he said aggressively, but he offered no explanation. He still held my arm and seemed to be trying to make up his mind what to do next.

"I won't tell anyone about you," I promised. "I give you my word."

"How do I know you'll keep it?" he demanded.

"Because I *say* I will. And you'll have to trust me," I said impatiently. "You can't watch me night and day. And besides when I'm missed, people will come looking for me and they're sure to find us. You don't want that I'm sure."

"I suppose you're right, I'll have to trust you," he replied, "but I've never really trusted anyone, not for a long time anyway, do you really promise?"

"Cross my heart," I said.

He let go of my arm then and I stood looking at him, wishing I could see him more clearly but it was impossible in that gloom. I wanted to hear more about him. He puzzled me, mystery surrounded him, and in spite of the fright he had given me there was something rather appealing about him.

There was no earthly reason why I should care what became of him but somehow already I felt almost involved.

"D'you need any help, food or anything?" I asked casually, half hoping he'd say yes.

"No. I can manage," he said shortly and turned away from me.

I left him then, glad to escape out into the light again, and had started along the path toward Mariners when I discovered that my purse was not in my pocket. It must have fallen out during the struggle in the cave. I turned and went quickly back, calling softly to him so that he would know it was only me.

"I've dropped my purse, do you see it anywhere?" I asked.

"Yes," he answered from the dimness of the inner cave—he evidently didn't intend that I should see him clearly. "I found it on the floor. Here, catch!"

He threw it toward me and I caught it. "Thanks," I said and walked away.

Then a thought struck me and I stopped to look inside it. I had had three one-pound notes, now there was only one.

I ran back into the cave blazing with anger.

"You rotten thief!" I shouted. "Why did you have to *take* my money? Couldn't you have told me when I asked you if you needed anything?"

"It was too good a chance to miss," he mumbled. "I've come to the end of mine but it doesn't matter, I'll get what I need, steal it if I have to—here, take your blasted money back and clear out."

He held the notes out to me and I took them.

"How long have you been hiding here?" I asked.

He paid no attention, so I repeated my question.

"Two days," he muttered unwillingly.

"Then you must have come to the end of your food supply. You don't have to steal. I'll get you what you need," I said, surprising myself by my offer. "Tell me what you want, and I'll buy it in the shop for you."

"Why should you?" he asked. "I can't pay you back, you know."

"That's O.K.," I assured him, "you can tell me about yourself instead and why you are here. Now, what shall I get? Can you cook, heat things up?"

"Oh yes, I bought a small outfit. I can heat soup or coffee and I can fry. I bought a sleeping bag too. That's how my money went so fast. I knew I'd have to camp out somewhere. It was a piece of luck finding this place—I didn't have to pinch any of this stuff," he added reassuringly. "I've been saving up all my pocket money for some time."

I nodded. "I'll get sausages and bread and apples and butter," I said, "and maybe a can of beans, and soup cubes and dried milk. What else—oh eggs, of course, and Nescafé. When shall I bring them to you?"

"I can manage on what I've got left till tomorrow morning," he said.

"O.K. I'll buy the stuff tonight and hide it till I bring ..."

"No one must know it's for me," he interrupted.

"Of course not," I said. I turned to go feeling quite excited, then I thought of something.

"We ought to have some kind of signal so that you'll know it's me," I suggested.

"What about whistling a tune—John Peel?" he whistled the first line.

"No, it's too well known, anyone might whistle it," I said. "What about—Bobby Shafto? D'you know it?" I whistled it through while he mouthed the words:

"Bobby Shafto's gone to sea,
Silver buckles at his knee,
He'll come back and marry me
Pretty Bobby Shafto."

"O.K." he said quite cheerfully, "Bobby Shafto it is."

"I'll be off then," I said and walked away.

"Harriet!" he called after me, "get me some matches and candles?"

"All right," I promised, "I'll bring them tomorrow and I won't say a word to anyone."

I walked slowly back to Mariners thinking over my adventure. I had given my word. I could not tell anyone, but I knew very well that I ought to do so. This boy was in trouble, he needed help whatever he had done. I would have to persuade him to let me tell the Mariners. I felt I was deceiving them by keeping silent. And I still didn't wholly understand why I had done what I did. Loneliness, I guessed, and wanting someone my own age to talk to.

I had a cup of tea with Mrs. Mariner in the kitchen and then I made an excuse to go up to the village to mail a letter.

"Take two of mine to mail with yours will you?" said Mrs. Mariner. "And when you get back the doctor says you can pop your head round Nancy's door for a few minutes."

"Oh good," I cried, "she must really be better. I won't be long."

I took a canvas bag with me to the shop and filled it with the food I had promised and the candles and matches. I added a few things like chocolate and cheese and biscuits and a piece of soap. When I had posted the letters I staggered back through the village, not even stopping to call in at Gramma's on the way, so frightened was I of being noticed and questioned, then I hurried down the hill.

I hid the bag in the gardener's shed just inside the gate of Mariners, hanging it from a strong nail in case mice got at the food. I decided it would be quite safe there till the morning.

When I went into the house, the lights were on and I appreciated the comfort and warmth that drew me inside.

I hung my anorak on a peg by the kitchen and pulled off my boots.

"May I come up?" I called.

"Yes, come on," Nancy's voice answered as her mother opened the door.

"Not for too long," whispered Mrs. Mariner as I reached the doorway of Nancy's room. "I'll leave you together," she said going on downstairs. "I'll be in my studio if you want me."

"*Well!*" I exclaimed leaning against the door jamb just outside the room, "how good to see you again, Nancy! Are you really feeling better? I do hope so."

I scrutinized her carefully. Her face was thin, and she was very pale, her skin had a sort of transparent look—she must have been pretty ill I thought.

"Oh I've decided to go on living for a bit longer," Nancy declared laughing, "but this disease is no joke, it leaves one feeling so weak, as if all one's stuffing had been removed. But to tell me, how are *you* getting on? D'you like it here? Are you finding enough to do?"

"Oh yes," I responded eagerly. "I miss you, of course,

but all kinds of exciting things have been happening to me."

"Oh? What for example?" Nancy asked. "Do tell."

I hesitated for a moment then I told her about the bats in the cave, and by the time I had finished my story her face was quite flushed with excitement and her laughter seemed perilously near to tears—to my consternation I realized that I had exhausted her. I had never been really ill myself, so I simply had not understood how easily one tired.

"I'd better go now," I said apologetically, "try to get strong again soon. I'll come to see you tomorrow if your mother lets me. 'Bye."

I went into my room to change my pullover and brush my hair, and my mood was thoughtful.

I could expect no advice or support from Nancy; she was not yet strong enough to be burdened with confidences, even those I was free to tell her. I felt very much on my own and not at all self-reliant. I wished I knew what to do about the boy, about Birney. If he was in trouble with the police, I certainly ought to tell someone, yet how could I break my promise to him? I did not want the responsibility of keeping his secret, but something about him roused my protective instinct in spite of his hostility.

Still puzzling over him I went down to the empty kitchen and picked up fat old Dowager. I settled her on my knee in the rocking chair and began to rock backward and forward, finding some comfort in the contact with the purring cat.

Chapter Ten

I could hardly wait to finish my breakfast and help with the chores next morning, so impatient was I to get down to the cave and deliver the food to Birney.

Mr. Mariner for once was in no hurry; he sat on smoking his pipe, his nose buried in his newspaper, his hand automatically feeling for his coffee cup till I thought I would burst with impatience.

Mrs. Mariner was upstairs attending to Nancy, and it was my job to clear away the breakfast things and wash them up.

At last he took his pipe out of his mouth and put down his paper.

"Well, Harriet, I'll be off. What are you going to be up to today?" he said conversationally, expecting no answer. "Better not go too far afield, weather's breaking, we'll get a blow most likely before nightfall, bound to get some rough weather, Candlemas was mild as May, means the worst of the winter is still to come."

He spoke with the authority of local knowledge and I believed him.

I fairly whisked the dishes off the table and had them washed and dried in no time.

I ran upstairs and popped my head round Nancy's door.

"I'm going for a run on the beach," I said. "I won't be very long."

Nancy groaned. "I wish I had one-eighth of your energy," she said.

I waited till Mrs. Pyke had arrived, and when she and Mrs. Mariner were absorbed with one another in the kitchen, I slipped out unobserved.

I went straight to the gardener's shed, got hold of the bag and was off down the path to the cove.

When I reached the cliffs, I hung about for a few minutes near the cave, but there was no one about that I could see so I whistled the first two lines of our signal tune, "Bobby Shafto," and waited.

Back to me came the next two lines, better whistled than mine. "Harriet? Come in!" whispered a husky voice out of the gloom before me, and I carefully picked my way through the outer cave lugging the heavy bag. He didn't offer to help me, and I dumped it at his feet. "There you are," I said.

"Got everything?" asked Birney. "O.K. . . . thanks."

He stood rather awkwardly waiting for me to go. I hadn't expected this and I felt a bit peeved. "Can't I come in?" I asked.

"I suppose so," he replied without enthusiasm. "Wait till I find a candle, you'll probably fall over something."

"I have my flashlight," I retorted, and I turned it on, but I felt there'd be a shrinking back from me on his part, so I had the sense not to light up his face. Instead I looked at his cave, and its grim bareness made me shudder. At least its walls and floor seemed reasonably dry unlike some of the other caves in which a constant drip could be heard, even a trickle at times, useful as a water supply though.

His sleeping bag lay along one wall and beside it his cooking kit and a pan. His place was really just a bulge or alcove in the inner cave, part of the tunnel that ran back into the hillside. It was drafty and bleak and could be bitterly cold, I thought, when the weather changed.

"Birney, you can't go on living here," I told him. "They're expecting a spell of stormy weather, Mr. Mariner said so. It'll be unbearable in here."

"It's safe," he said shortly, "I hope."

"Why do you have to hide?" I asked. "What have you done?"

"Nothing that matters to you," he snapped.

"You're wrong, it does matter to me," I said. "I got these things for you, and now I'm involved too."

His knees seemed to give way suddenly and he sat

61

down on a chunk of rock and began to mutter as if he were talking to himself.

"What a hopeless mess I've made," he murmured and there was a kind of despair in his voice. "I just don't know where to go from here."

He sat huddled in misery. It was not the reaction I had expected. I didn't know what to say, but at that moment I ached with compassion for him whatever he had done.

"Don't be so down," I whispered, "It can't be as bad as all that. Won't you tell me? I promise I'll not split on you, you really *can* trust me."

I don't know why I said that. Against my will almost, I was involving myself more deeply in the troubles of this strange boy, but I couldn't help it for somehow Birney had begun to matter to me.

Resentfully he shrugged.

"You'd better go," he said, "I can't tell you anything— not now anyway. I'll have to think about it first. I'm hungry. I'm going to have something to eat." He didn't offer me anything so I took an apple from my pocket and began to munch it. "Go ahead," I said.

He lit one of the candles and unwrapping the bread I had brought he broke off a wedge, buttered it and sat down again, keeping in the shadows.

"Why don't we both go outside?" I suggested for I hated the gloom of his cave and the flickering candle. "It's not much of a day, pretty gray and overcast actually, but we could get into the daylight?"

"No," he objected. "I can't risk it now, only after dark, someone might see me."

"But there's no one about," I protested, "not a soul, at this time of year."

He looked at me, suddenly alert and somehow wary.

"That's what *you* think," he said quietly.

We ate in silence for a few minutes while I thought about him. He seemed more relaxed, less aggressive, but he did not yet fully trust me; he did not want me to see him properly, and the more he hid his face from me, the more I longed to see it.

After a while I got up. "I'd better go now," I said. "Is there anything else you need?"

He shook his head. "I'm O.K." he grunted.

"Shall I come back again later if I can?" I asked.

"If you want to," he replied noncommittally.

"What will you find to do all day?" I asked.

"Explore the caves, sleep a bit, eat, think perhaps—oh I need a penknife. I must have dropped mine somewhere," he explained.

My mind flashed back again to the boy I had thought was a ghost, had it really been Birney? I felt there was some significant connection between the two boys, Ambrose Briddle and Birney, but I could not think what it was.

"I'll try to get a knife for you and bring it next time I come," I promised.

"O.K." he mumbled, then just before I was out of earshot, "Harriet . . . thanks," he called.

I felt absurdly pleased.

At lunchtime I asked Mr. Mariner if he had an old penknife I could have, one that he didn't want.

"What d'you need a knife for? Taking stones out of horses' shoes no doubt," he said, teasing me.

"And corks out of bottles," I joked back. He produced

an old knife from a drawer in his desk, and it had every-thing, even a can opener.

"You can keep this one," he said.

I thanked him and put it in my jeans pocket—I would deliver it later.

Mrs. Mariner was in the studio struggling to finish a painting, and Nancy, when I peeped round her door, was obviously very drowsy, so I decided to do some school-work for an hour before I went out again. I hauled out my books and spread them on my dressing table, but I found it difficult to concentrate, my mind was too rest-less. The wind was rising, little tappings, knockings, un-easy crackings kept disturbing me, and out at sea the sky was lowering, ominous, with great black storm clouds massing. There was a feeling of portent in the air, a gathering of the natural forces for battle.

"I'll go up to Gramma's," I said aloud, and I bundled my books back into the cupboard, pulled on my anorak, called a hasty good-bye to Nancy, and opened the front door. There I hesitated for a minute, looking out from the safety of the house to the threatening landscape. For a moment I felt daunted, loath to leave the security of this home where I had a sense of belonging and my own accepted place to face what lay outside, the sinister un-dertones of a hidden world beyond my reach.

But I pulled myself together and stepped boldly out onto the path that led to Gramma's cottage and the village.

Chapter Eleven

The wind racing behind me blew me up the hill toward
Gramma's cottage. When I reached it, I knocked loudly
on the door and went in, just managing to avoid stepping
on a large toad that was squatting on the mat immediately
inside.

"Ugh!" I squealed startled. "Gramma, there's a toad
in the house! Shall I put it out?"

"Oh 'er?" Gramma shouted back. "No leave 'er be, 'er
always comes in for company when storm's a-brewin'.
'Er does no harm, 'er's a friendly creature."

65

I walked carefully past the toad and into the kitchen.

Gramma was seated in her usual chair, her wire spectacles perched on her nose, she wore her fur cap without the balaclava and her crinkled old hands worked slowly at a crocheted square of yellow wool, for a blanket I supposed.

"Put kettle on, Harriet, we'll have a cup o' tea, but ye'll have to get it, me joints be creakin' somethin' cruel today," she explained. "I bin sittin' here quite teary-eyed with pain."

When we were settled with our steaming cups, she eyed me over her glasses.

"What ye bin a-doin?" she inquired. "I haven't zeen ye since Candlemas. Did ye bide hwome then like I told ye?"

"Yes, I stayed inside after dark," I said, and she nodded satisfied. "But why did you warn me not to go out then?" I asked. "Was there some special reason?"

Gramma took off her glasses and set them on the table by her cup, then she put them on again and gave me a long deliberate look.

"Strange things do happen on that night," she said quietly. "There do be powerful forces about like I told ye avore. There be zome that would ill-wish ye and worse, if they thought ye'd been a-watchin' them. Remember the boy who were drowned, after Candlemas."

I did indeed remember him, my poor ghost I had seen on the beach that night—or had it been Birney? I also remembered the pattering of feet going past in the night, the murmuring voices, the trampled grass round the ruins of the chapel, the ashes of the fire inside its walls.

"D'you mean that *now*, in the twentieth century,

they'd really try to harm anyone who watched them?"
I asked in disbelief.

"Zertain zure they would," said Gramma, "zertain as
they drowned that poor boy."

"But *did* they drown him, wasn't it just an accident?
How can you know for certain?" I asked.

"Because my Grannie were there, she were one o'
them. She told me so herself when she were a wold
'ooman after she quit the coven."

"You mean she was a *witch?*" I gasped. "Good grief!
Why did she quit?"

Gramma leaned toward me and lowered her voice as
she went on. "Because she grew too scared after that
boy's death. She had no part in it mind, but her con-
science troubled 'er, she never got over it, never. I lived
wi' her, see, and she told me all about it. Woonce she
even did show me their staff, but she'd never have let
me join *them* even if I'd a-wanted to." Gramma shivered
slightly. " 'Tis a wold story now and best forgotten," she
murmured, glancing over her shoulder as if she might
be overheard.

"Showed you the staff?" I repeated overcome with
new curiosity. "What staff?"

"A queer wold stick of black wood, carved wi' ani-
mals' heads, cats and toads and vipers and such like. My
Grannie never did know where it come from nor how it
come to be in the village, but special it were and only
used at the four great sabbats, very highly thought of it
were by *them*, the symbol like of the coven, the root of
their evil power."

"And you actually saw it, Gramma? Where?" I asked.

"Here in this wold house where I do zit, which were

hers long avore it were mine, ye see. Kep' it for a year, she did, hidden zomewhere under this roof, zaid it were her turn to house it, she did. 'Tis gone long since o' course, *I* never did zee it again and maybe no one knows about it no more, but a dreadful fearsome thing it were."

I refilled her teacup, and when she picked it up I noticed that her hand was shaking so that the tea slopped into the saucer. That decided me.

"I heard *them* on Candlemas night, Gramma," I confided. "I heard them going down past Mariners in the dark, and I found the grass trampled next day all round the little chapel and the ashes of a fire inside it."

Gramma looked at me frowning.

"Then, ye'd do well to forget it," she said tartly. "Take good care to know nothin' about it, have nothin' to do wi' *them*, 'tis too dangerous. I knows who they are and I knows what I'm a-talking about. They're the outcasts of the village like, they don't belong inside. Because of my Grannie bein' one o' *them*, I too were outside for years and years. Woonce you've bin outside it's hard to come in, hard to forgive them that's kep' you out. Even now, ordinary volks be scared o' me a little! But I don't care no more," she cackled, "there be good company both outside and in, and I'm a-nearin' the end o' my journey anyways."

In a little while I left her, for I wanted to get back to Mariners to take the penknife to Birney before it got dark. As I ran down the path from the village, I kept thinking about what Gramma had told me, and I wondered how much of it to believe. Even if there was some truth in what Mrs. Mariner had said about the old woman's stories, even if some of them were only dramas of her own imagination, even if I felt partly skeptical about what Gramma had told me, I could not help wondering.

I went straight past Mariners and on down the path toward the beach, battling my way against the strengthening wind till I came to the edge of the cliffs and the desolate hollows of the caves.

I whistled my lines of our signal tune and waited, then the rest was whistled by Birney and I went in.

"The penknife," I said holding it out to him, "and he doesn't want it back."

"Who doesn't? You didn't say it was for me?" he asked suspicious at once.

"I did not, Mr. Mariner thought it was for me," I replied. "Are you all right? I can't see you properly. *Surely* you can trust me by now, can't we have some light?"

"No," said Birney, aggressive at once, "it's easier to talk in the dark."

My spirits lifted a little, so he *was* going to talk, to tell me about himself after all, but I sensed that I must be cautious and gentle and help him as much as I could if I did not want to put him right off.

"Go ahead," I said softly. "I'm listening. How do you come to be here?"

"Because I've run away," he muttered.

"From home or from school?" I asked.

"From an approved school," he replied. "Moorhill. I've been there for almost two years . . . on a criminal charge."

"A *criminal* charge?" I gasped. "I just don't believe it! Whatever did you do?"

"It's a long story," said Birney wearily, "you won't want to know me when you've heard it."

"Don't be so silly," I retorted, "whatever you've done

you must have had a good reason for doing it. Please tell me."

"It all started when my father died, four years ago." There was a long pause as if he felt it too painful to go on.

"How awful to lose your father," I prompted gently, "it must have been terrible for you and for your mother. I suppose she . . ."

"Not for her," he broke in, speaking in a hurt tone I'd never heard him use before. "It didn't seem to matter to her. I can't understand how she could have forgotten him so soon."

"Whatever makes you think that?" I asked.

"Because she met someone else and they were married in less than a year," he said bitterly.

"Perhaps she couldn't bear the loneliness without him," I suggested.

There was another long pause while I thought how to encourage him to go on.

"What was your father? What did he do?" I asked.

"He was a gunnery officer in the navy," Birney replied. "He was killed in an accident on his ship."

"And your . . . stepfather?" I asked.

Birney nearly exploded with fury. "Don't call him that!" he shouted, forgetting caution, "he's a rotten type . . . she'd be much better without him . . . I hate and despise him . . . I loathe him and his filthy money. He's changed my mother, corrupted her so that I don't know her anymore. She doesn't care about me. Oh what's the use of telling you, you'll never understand."

"I'm certainly beginning to understand why you are here," I said quietly. "What did you do to him?"

"I stole from him. I stole again and again. But he wouldn't be provoked into fighting with me, he wouldn't even punish me. He just forgave me and tried to make friends. Somehow that made me hate him more than ever . . . then I tried to kill him. I tried to wreck his car when he was alone in it. I know quite a bit about cars and I found out just what to do."

"But you didn't succeed?"

"No. I failed. He only broke his leg not his miserable neck. I wish I'd been able to try again," said Birney viciously.

I was appalled, sickened and shocked by what he had tried to do. But I made myself appear cool.

"So you were sent to an approved school. How long have you been there?" I asked.

"Almost two years," he said. "I'll be leaving soon, then I'll have a year under care."

"If you've nearly finished your time there, why did you run away? It seems a stupid thing to do so near the end," I remarked.

"I had a letter from my mother . . . that upset me," he mumbled.

"But doesn't she come to see you? She can't just have forgotten you?" I insisted.

"They live in Canada now," he explained, "but she writes now and then, stiff cold little letters that are worse than useless—then in this one she told me that she's going to have a baby, *his* baby . . . and I couldn't stand it. It sent me crazy."

"So that's why you ran away!" I exclaimed. "That on top of everything else was too much for you . . . you sort of lost your head. Poor Birney, you must love her very much. But surely there was someone you could have told, talked to about it I mean, a matron or a master or a friend?"

"There's no one. No one cares. They're all out to punish me for what I did. I've never talked to *anyone*, anyone but you since—it happened."

I was appalled not only at what he had done, or tried to do, but also at the terrible unhappiness he must have suffered to have been driven to such desperate lengths.

"We've got to think hard what to do, what would be best for you," I said.

"*We?*" he queried.

"Oh yes, we! I'm in it too, I told you that" I said.

"Nonsense!" he retorted. "You don't know what you're saying. Just mind your own business." Then he went on in a quieter tone. "There's nothing to be done. It's hopeless. What I did has put me outside decent society, everybody says so. You'd better forget you ever met me. I'm utterly sunk. Finished."

Suddenly as if all the life had drained out of him, he slumped back against the rock.

"Go away," he gulped.

Fierce pity welled up in me making my throat ache. I did not move while he struggled to get control of himself, but eventually I went close to him and put my arms round him. I wanted to show him that someone did care.

Chapter Twelve

By this time the wind had strengthened and was blowing half a gale, and it had become much colder in the cave. Under the cliffs the waves boomed and thundered as they rushed into cracks and blowholes at sea level. The noise reverberated through the old quarries like blasts from a gun.

"Birney, do let me tell someone and get help for you," I begged. "I can't just walk off and leave you here alone like this. The storm is getting worse too, you'll be frozen in this drafty spot. And they'll find you in the end, you know."

"No," he said firmly, "you're not to tell anyone. You promised."

I was silent for a minute then I sighed.

"All right," I agreed reluctantly, "I won't say anything, not yet, but do think again seriously. I know I can find help for you, from people who'll understand, like the Mariners. And even if you have to go back to that school for a bit, it isn't the end, you know. Look, wrap yourself up in your sleeping bag and try to keep warm. I won't be able to come again till Monday. Will you be all right till then? Mr. Mariner will be at home tomorrow, so I'll have to be there, and there are often people about down here on a Sunday, so you'd better stay hidden. It wouldn't be safe for me to come to you. D'you understand?" He nodded but he scarcely noticed when I left, he seemed sunk in despair, listless, lifeless almost. I felt afraid to leave him lest the feeble flame that still flickered in him might be snuffed out in the night. But I knew I must go, the Mariners would be worried if I stayed out any longer.

I took a grip on myself and forced my way along the cliff's edge and up the path toward the house. Great crested waves pounded the beach; the roar and rush of the water combined with the howling wind to make a scene of desolation.

I reached the house and managed to get the door shut against the storm. I pulled off my anorak and popped my head round the kitchen door.

"I'll be with you in a moment," I said to Mrs. Mariner.

"I just want to change then I'll look in on Nancy for a minute if I may."

I dashed up the stairs, changed my damp sweater and jeans, had a quick wash and knocked on Nancy's door.

Remembering her exhaustion of the previous evening, I stopped in the doorway only for a minute or two, commenting on the gathering of the storm.

"It's fierce down in the cove," I told her, "you can hardly stand against the wind, and the waves are enormous. It's a wonderful feeling to come out of it into the warmth and peace of the house."

"I love a storm," Nancy confessed. "It's exciting and primitive and seems to cut through the top dressing of convention to the basic essentials of life, if you see what I mean."

"Yes, I do," I answered, "but I think I'd rather see it from some safe shelter." And I thought of Birney and shivered.

The house seemed doubly welcoming that night. I felt cherished, guarded, and although the fury of the storm prevented me from hearing any other sound, I had a feeling that the wind had carried our winged guardians home to their vigil over Mariners. It was a comforting thought.

Supper was a long drawn-out meal because Mr. Mariner was very late getting in, and Mrs. Mariner and I started and then sat talking while we waited for him. At last he arrived, and he had just settled to the meal, which had been kept hot for him, when we turned on the radio for the news. First there was a police message giving a short description of a missing boy, aged sixteen, who had absconded from Moorhill Approved School. Would anyone recognizing him please inform the police at once —Birney!

I felt myself go scarlet and then white with shock—the announcement had caught me off guard. I suppose I should have expected something of the sort. However no one seemed to notice me.

"Poor little blighter, I hope he's hiding indoors tonight," Mr. Mariner remarked thoughtfully as he ate his stew. I thought again of Birney shivering in his hole in the cliff, and I felt terribly tempted to blurt out the whole story there and then, but I had given Birney my word and he trusted me to keep my promise. I felt it was tremendously important that he should be able to trust *someone*, so I said nothing.

I kept my bedroom windows shut when I went to bed, but the gale battered and rattled at them all night long, and I got little sleep. I lay worrying about Birney, trying to make up my mind what to do. Somehow I had to persuade him to release me from my promise and get help for him.

When Monday morning came, it was as wild as ever, and Mr. Mariner warned me to keep away from the cliffs. But how could I? I had to see that Birney was all right. As soon as I'd done my chores I filled a thermos with hot coffee and slipped out. It was hard work making my way down to the cove against the gale. The whole landscape was dark, menacing, and I saw that the wind was driving heavy rain clouds straight for us.

When I reached the caves, it was impossible to make my feeble whistling of our tune heard above the crash and howl of wave and wind, but Birney must have been looking out for me and actually seemed relieved to see me. He was much more cheerful than he had been on Saturday evening so I did not tell him at once about the police message. I did not want to deflate him again.

"Hallo Birney!" I greeted him, shouting above the wind, "How did you get on those two nights? Did you sleep at all? Was it very awful?"

"It depends what you mean by awful," he spoke into my ear. "Nothing could be so awful to me as going back to Moorhill, but it was pretty rough I must say."

"Was Moorhill so specially awful?" I asked. "Why?"

"The other boys," he explained, "some of them are decent enough, but the leaders, or barons as we call them, are cowardly thugs and bullies and make everyone's life a misery."

"But there are masters, why don't they stop the bullying?" I asked.

"Because they can't, or they don't know about it. Most of it goes on after dark when we are locked in for the night, then the barons take over."

"Can't one of you tell the headmaster what goes on?" I suggested.

"Anyone who dared to might meet with a very nasty accident," said Birney bitterly. "He'd be badly beaten up, perhaps maimed for life. None of us is brave enough or foolish enough to even try."

A sudden blast of wind swirled its way round the cave with exceptional vigor, and I shivered. "How can you endure this?" I asked. "Did you get *any* sleep last night?"

"Not much, it was pretty drafty—and cold too," Birney acknowledged. "It might be a good idea to explore a

77

bit this morning and try to find a more sheltered place in the inner cave. Did you bring a flashlight?"

"Yes, I've got it here," I shouted and without thinking I turned it on. It caught him full in the face, a pale face crowned with a head of tousled dark hair. He was not a violent thuggish type at all, there was nothing repellent in his looks now that I could see him properly. There was no brutality in his intelligent face, only a closed look like one who has suffered deeply. His gray eyes regarded me steadily, and I wanted more than ever to help him. I liked very much what I saw.

Quickly I shifted the beam to the roof, expecting a rebuke, but he said nothing.

"Which way shall we try first?" I asked.

"Maybe one of the side caves, further into the hill," he said.

"O.K. you lead," I suggested, handing him the flashlight, and stooping followed him along a narrow tunnel that led from his cave into the hillside.

Presently the passage opened out into a high chamber which was divided into an upper and a lower room, like a small hall with a minstrel's gallery.

"This is better, warmer and quieter," said Birney cheerfully, and I noticed that the sounds of wind and sea had subsided into a sort of sobbing—it seemed a good hideout.

Birney clambered to the upper chamber, the gallery, while I shone the flashlight, then he took it and gave me a hand up.

It was quite a small place, low ceilinged, sheltered, and completely dry, deep inside the cliff. He really could be quite snug up here, compared with his first hideout. There was a long low slab of rock raised off the ground, which he could use as a bed, and there were several little natural shelves in the walls of rock on which he could stow his gear.

"It's good, isn't it?" I said enthusiastically. "Shall we move your things up here?"

Birney was poking round searching with the flashlight, making a careful examination before he committed himself. While I waited I was wondering how I could get him to talk about giving himself up, for I knew I must soon tell him about the police message on the radio.

Suddenly he chuckled and gave a low whistle. "Look, Harriet!" he exclaimed excitedly. "Look what I've found!"

I hurried across to where he was shining the flashlight and bent over the stone bed slab to look—in a niche behind the slab and hidden by it, lay a stick of polished black wood, a stick curiously carved all over, carved with animal heads.

"Birney!" I gasped, "it's the staff, it belongs to *them*, to the witches of the village. It's the symbol of their power, their magic. Don't touch it! It's evil and dangerous."

"What on earth are you talking about—it sounds sheer nonsense!" snorted Birney derisively, and he picked the stick up in his hand and held it under the light to examine it thoroughly.

"It's certainly beautiful and curious!" he exclaimed. But what makes you think it has magic powers? Who told you?"

So I repeated to him what Gramma had told me.

"There's a group in the village who practice witchcraft, a coven," I explained. "I heard them in the night,

I heard them passing Mariners on their way to the cove—to celebrate Candlemas."

"So that's what they were doing!" exclaimed Birney amused. "I heard them too, I even watched them walking in a procession with burning flares from the caves to the old ruin down there in the cove. I couldn't make out what on earth they were up to, and of course I kept well out of sight. One of them must have slipped back into the cave to hide the staff when it was all over."

"Are you certain none of them saw you?" I asked anxiously. "For if any of them know you were watching, you may be in great danger."

"What do you mean?" he scoffed. "What possible harm could they do to me—beyond telling the police?"

Then I told him Gramma's story of the boy who was drowned, after Candlemas.

"Whew!" he said. "Is that really true? She's pretty old isn't she, don't you think she may have imagined it all?"

I shook my head.

"I don't think so, she's quite certain about it, and although she was only a small child when the boy was drowned, she remembers vividly what her grandmother told her about it later on, when she was shown the staff, and discovered that her grandmother was one of the witches and had seen it all. That's something that would frighten and impress a child too much ever to be forgotten."

"Well, thanks for the warning," said Birney lightly, "though I don't think anyone saw me, and in any case that drowning happened years and years ago. Things are different now, witchcraft is finished, dead."

"Don't be too sure of that," I said. "The staff still exists, the 'root of their evil power,' Gramma called it. It may still be dangerous. Evil is neither finished nor dead."

"Well, *we've* got the staff now," said Birney grinning, "perhaps we should try a bit of magic with it ourselves."

He took it all very lightheartedly I thought, and he began twirling the staff around like a drum-major's baton. I felt I must stop him and I put out my hand to take it from him.

But before I could grasp it, I recoiled in horror and disbelief, for it seemed to vibrate with a life of its own, it rippled with movement—like a snake.

"Put it down, Birney!" I cried. "It's alive! It's horrible —someone ought to destroy it, to burn it. I never want to see it again!"

Birney must have understood that it had really scared and upset me, for without a word he laid it back in its niche. In spite of his skepticism I noticed that after touching it he wiped his hand carefully on the seat of his jeans.

Chapter Thirteen

"Well, what about it," I asked, "are you going to move into this inner cave? It's much safer and less cold. Shall I help you?"

"I don't know," he said hesitating, "suppose someone comes for the staff and finds me here."

"I don't think anyone will come. Gramma says it is very special and is only used four times a year. The next time isn't for three months. They'll probably leave it hidden here till May," I said.

"O.K. I'll risk it. Let's move my gear at once. I can

probably stay safely here for a bit," Birney spoke quite cheerfully, "if you'll go on getting food for me."

"Birney—why don't you give yourself up now. *Please*," I said earnestly. "I'm only here till school reopens in about another week."

"A lot can happen in a week," said Birney.

"I know, that's what frightens me," I retorted. "Even if you won't give yourself up to the police, at least let me tell Mr. Mariner. He's a splendid person, and I know he'd help you to get out of the mess you're in."

"*No*," said Birney quite fiercely, "you've got to keep your promise not to tell anyone. They'll only send me back to that Moorhill place again. I think I'd rather be dead."

I waited for a moment till he calmed down.

"O.K." I said. "I promised. But Birney, I've got to tell you there was a police message on the radio on Saturday night, giving a description of you."

"Did it say where I might be?" he asked, "where people should be on the lookout for me?"

"No, I don't think so, but a message like that does alert everyone," I pointed out.

"Well, they don't know where to look yet—the police I mean—it may be ages before they find me."

"And what good will that do you?" I demanded. "You're certain to be caught in the end."

"I can cause a good deal of trouble before they catch me," he said angrily, "and why shouldn't I? I owe society nothing, they've thrown me out, remember?"

"That's very silly, be your age," I said crossly. "*You* put yourself outside by what you did. There's no sense in getting into even worse trouble. You'll have to face up to the fact that you can't go on hiding for much longer. Surely it's time you started to plan what you're going to do?"

"That's just the trouble," Birney explained. "I don't know—I can't plan. I've been shut away for too long. I'm used to being *told* what to do. I can't plan for myself anymore, I haven't the courage."

"What nonsense!" I cried. "Of course you've got courage, you've *shown* me you have. And you planned to run away and did it. It's only that you are undecided, unsure of yourself. You've paid for what you did, you've been punished, now you can put it behind you and make a new start. You can't want to go on living like this, like an outcast. But you must make up your own mind. *Please*, Birney, get help and give yourself a chance, *please* let me talk to Mr. Mariner."

"Once and for all, NO," said Birney and he turned his back on me, so I just left him and stalked off angrily. But as I reached the outer cave and met the full blast of the wind, I heard him shout, so I waited. He came out toward me from the inner cave and spoke into my ear.

"Could you borrow something for me to read d'you think? A couple of paperbacks or even a newspaper? I spend so much of my time thinking about my problems that I need some distraction."

"I'll see what I can do," I said rather grudgingly. "I'll try to bring them before the rain comes. I don't want to get drenched."

"I'll be in the inner cave," said Birney, ". . . thanks, Harriet."

He grinned at me so endearingly that my good humor

was restored and I went almost lightheartedly up the hill to Mariners.

"I'm going to the village before the rain comes," I told Mrs. Mariner, popping my head round the door of the studio. "Is there anything I can get for you?"

"Oh—Harriet—yes thanks," she mumbled absently, then wrenching her attention away from her painting for a moment, "There's a list as long as your arm in the kitchen, leave it at the shop, there's a dear, and tell them I'll collect the order this afternoon. And pop the local paper in to Gramma when you're passing, will you?"

"O.K." I said. "I won't be long."

"Nancy!" I called up the stairs, "is there anything you want from the village?"

"Only some more knitting wool and you won't get it here," Nancy shouted. So I picked up the paper for Gramma and the list for the shop and went off.

As I hurtled up the hill before the wind and thought over the events of the morning, the finding of the inner cave, the discovery of the witch staff, and Birney's impossible situation, my earlier cheerfulness dimmed. I felt trapped, caught in a net of trouble and anxiety not of my own making, and I hadn't a notion how to break out of it.

I went to the shop first and gave Mrs. Mariner's order, and I bought a bar of mint chocolate for Nancy. Then I made for Gramma's cottage, but as I passed the church, on a sudden impulse I stepped inside and sat down. It was empty and serene and beautiful, with a quietness that hushed my misgivings. The candles were all gone, but a bowl of white flowers stood before the altar. I sat for a few minutes absorbing the peace and when I rose to leave I felt strengthened and reassured.

Gramma's geese announced my arrival with screechings that vied with the wind in violence. I knocked at the cottage door and went in, stepping carefully where I expected the toad to be, but he wasn't there.

I found Gramma kneeling before her fire, wrestling with a downward draft which swirled the smoke round the room instead of up the chimney. Her cap was crooked, her face smudged with ash, and she was swearing angrily.

"I've brought you the paper," I said, "with Mrs. Mariner's compliments."

"Drat that wind!" muttered Gramma as another cloud of smoke filled the room, making our eyes smart. "Here girl, hold one end of this wold paper till the vire gets a-goin'," she ordered.

I knelt beside her on the hearth holding one side of the newspaper, which was stretched tautly across the fire, while Gramma held the other side, till the sound of crackling as the flames caught the sticks showed that the fire was well away at last.

"That's better, now help me up," said Gramma and I heaved her up off the floor and eased her into her chair.

"Now put the kettle on," she commanded, "and let's have a chat." She was really in a bossy mood!

"It's nearly lunchtime," I pointed out, "and they'll be expecting me back. I mustn't stay long."

"Well, ye can spare us a minute or two—what's to do?" she asked, avid for news as usual.

"Nothing much, Nancy's feeling a bit better and Mr. Mariner says there's a storm coming. Oh—and Gramma—

I found the witch staff, the one you told me about. It's hidden in one of the old quarry caves by the sea."

Gramma looked startled. "So it's still about," she whispered. "I might 'a known it. That's wot keeps *them* goin', without that wold stick there'd be no power, see."

"You mean if the staff were to be destroyed there would be no more witchcraft in the village?"

"That's right, but no one would dare do it, it's too dangerous," said Gramma. "I 'spect *I'll* have to pay for even havin' told ye about it. Now, listen to me, Harriet, forget ye ever found that wold staff, just put the whole thing out o' yer mind."

"I'll try," I promised, but it wasn't the most important thing I had on my mind. There was Birney, Birney who leaned on me as his one trusted link with normality, Birney whose whole future surely depended on what I did or did not do. The burden of responsibility was beginning to get me down. I longed to tell somebody, somebody older and wiser than myself. I wondered how much longer I would have to hold out on my own.

As I rose to go, there was the sound of heavy boots on the doorstep, followed by a loud tapping and a cheerful voice shouting, "Anyone at home?" and into the room stepped the village policeman.

Gramma regarded him stonily.

"G'mornin' Mrs. Cobbley, mornin' Miss," he said turning to me, then he took off his helmet and sat down beside Gramma.

"Wot be you wantin' wi' me, Bob Parkin?" demanded Gramma.

"Jest a call in passing, Mrs. Cobbley," said the policeman in a conciliatory tone. "Since you live alone like, I wanted to make sure you was all right."

"Why shouldn't I be all right?" asked Gramma. "As you see I've got Nancy Mariner's friend here for company."

"You're visitin' the Mariners, Miss? I heard they had a guest," said Bob Parkin, "and I'm told Miss Nancy is ill?"

"Yes," I answered, "but she's getting better."

"There's been no one botherin' you then, Mrs. Cobbley, no vagrants knockin' at your door, no young lads beggin' food?" asked the policeman.

"No, none," said Gramma, "was ye lookin' for one?"

"Just keepin' me eyes and ears open," he said soothingly. "You'll let me know if anyone comes along?" he added.

"That depends," snapped Gramma. "Good day to ye, Bob Parkin."

He nodded to me, and as he rose to go the penny dropped and I realized that the inquiries he was making were about the boy who was missing, who had run away —about Birney.

Chapter Fourteen

The knowledge struck me like a blow, my knees began to shake as I tried to control my face, not to show the dismay I felt. I must get away from Gramma before her keen eye noticed that I was upset.

I jumped to my feet. "I'll have to go now," I cried, "take care of yourself, Gramma," and before she could say a word I dashed out of the door. She must have thought me very odd, but I dreaded her questioning me. I was terrified of giving something away that might endanger Birney. And yet, where would he find a better refuge than in Gramma's cottage, or a more sympathetic ear than hers—so long as she was in the right mood, although she *was* rather unpredictable. I did not really believe she would give Birney away if she knew about him, but I had made him a renewed promise of silence which I must keep.

I battled my way down the hill against the wind and just managed not to be late for lunch. Mr. Mariner had not arrived so we started without him, and when he did come in he bolted his food and was off again back to his quarries, where he had his hands full of trouble with a threatened strike by the truck drivers who moved the stone for him by road. I could see he was preoccupied and worried.

I helped to clear and wash up, and I threw Nancy the bar of chocolate I had got her and told her from her doorway about the policeman's visit to Gramma.

"Bob Parkin won't get much help from her, if there's someone on the run," commented Nancy, "and I bet he knows it and will keep a careful eye on her cottage."

I noted this piece of information and tucked it carefully away in a corner of my mind for future use, if necessary.

"What are you going to do?" Nancy asked. "I suppose I'd better take my afternoon nap like an obedient invalid—oh rot, I'm sick of being in bed!"

"Cheer up!" I said laughing. "You'll soon be back at school and wishing you were at home with glandular fever again! Better take your nap while you get the chance. I'm going out for a blast of air, and then I *must* get on with some more schoolwork."

I went into my bedroom where there was a shelf of

paperbacks. I chose two or three of them and put them in my shoulder bag, then once again I went off to visit Birney.

The first spots of rain began to fall as I left the house for the cove, and I pulled up the hood of my anorak and zipped it up to the neck. I had to struggle hard against the wind which was blowing fiercely by then. It took all my strength to reach the turning to the caves and to fight my way along the shelf above the cove.

A huge sea was running and the battering surge of the waves on the rocks seemed to shake the very foundations of the headland, so that I wondered whether the whole precarious structure of caves might disintegrate and crash down into the foam below.

I made my way over the boulders into the outer cave, then on through the tunnel, which led to the inner chamber and Birney's new hideout. Here it was comparatively sheltered from the noise of the gale and I was able to whistle our tune quite audibly. In a moment Birney's answering whistle reached me. I lit my flashlight and plunged on in, puzzled by the smell of smoke that met me.

He was waiting for me in the lower part of his new cave and up behind him his gear was arranged in the gallery. In the flickering candlelight it looked almost cozy and homelike.

"I've brought your books," I said and stopped dead. "What on earth have you been doing?" I asked. Birney stood looking down at a semicircle of gray ash at his feet and his expression was sheepish—it was also rather scared.

"I've burned it," he whispered. "It was really quite

extraordinary. As it caught fire it bent into a bow shape arching itself as if it were alive. It was really rather frightening."

"What *are* you talking about?" I asked completely baffled.

"The staff of course," he retorted. "That old witch staff."

"Oh Birney, what *have* you done?" I faltered.

"Only destroyed it. You said it frightened you and someone should burn it. You said you never wanted to see it again—I did it for *you*." he finished aggrieved.

His face was dejected, he expected praise and approval from me.

"It was marvelous of you, and brave," I said, "thank you, Birney. I'm terribly glad it has gone, forever."

He looked relieved, and I stifled my horror at the danger he had put himself into. What if the witches should discover their loss and find out who was responsible, discover who had been spying on them and remove him as they had removed that other boy long ago?

Just then I became aware of an intense stillness in the cave, a hush that unnerved me, the kind of eerie lull that sometimes comes in the middle of a storm. I was afraid to move, almost afraid to breathe. I stood listening intently, thinking of Gramma and what she had told me about the staff, remembering how her hand was trembling by the end of her story. Carefully I leaned toward the warm ash and touched it with my toe. A sudden loud crack split the silence and small splinters of stone began to rain down from the roof. I dodged out of their way covering my head with my arms. And at that instant, the ash on the floor rose in a spiral up into the air and swirled past me to the mouth of the cave, and out into the storm.

I gasped, and switched on my flashlight. Birney's hair seemed to be standing on end, and his face glistened with sweat.

"What——on earth——was that?" he gulped.

"I don't know. I don't know—but it's g-gone," I stammered, "whatever it was—it's gone. Over. Finished." We just stood and stared at one another, speechless and shaken.

Birney recovered his composure before I did. He took a deep breath and held out his hand to me.

"Come on and inspect my den," he invited. I clambered up after him from the lower cave into the gallery and sat down on his sleeping bag, which was spread out on the raised bed of stone.

"Anything to report?" he asked, "or is all still quiet?"

I told him then about the policeman's visit to Gramma and how she had held her own.

"Good for her," Birney remarked, "but I wonder if he's got any clue of my whereabouts to go on. You haven't given anyone a hint have you?"

"Certainly *not*," I said indignantly. "What do you take me for?"

"Well, sorry, but I'm a bit edgy what with the police hunt and this gale, and that wretched stick behaving so strangely. It was quite uncanny."

"It's O.K.," I replied. "In my opinion there is plenty to *be* edgy about, and scared too. I only hope you get away with the burning without any repercussions."

"What long words you use, Grandmama," teased Birney miming Red Ridinghood. "You must be pretty bright at school."

"I'm not bad at English, and I enjoy words," I said, "but I think I'd better get back to Mariners now in case that policeman turns up there and finds me out. He might come here looking for me. I'd better go. All right for food?"

"Yes thanks, till tomorrow anyway."

"O.K., enjoy the books and keep hidden," I advised. "See you tomorrow."

I drew up my hood again and scrambled out into the wind and the rain, which were now driving at me full force like a solid sheet of water. I ran up the path from the cove as fast as I could but even in the short distance before I reached Mariners I was drenched and frozen so that my teeth were chattering with cold.

Mrs. Mariner was coming downstairs as I burst in and exclaimed in disapproval at my state—"Good heavens, Harriet, what on earth possessed you to go out in this deluge?" she cried.

"I needed some fresh air before I settle down to my schoolwork for the rest of the day," I told her. "It was scarcely raining at all when I left, but it's frightful now."

She helped me to peel off my sodden clothing and carted it into the kitchen to be dried.

"You'd better have a hot bath straight away," she advised me, "we don't want you catching a chill."

I went upstairs and ran a bath, but by the time I got into it the water had run tepid so it didn't do me any good. I gave myself a good rub with my towel and got into warm dry clothing. Then I went into my room and shut the door and settled down to my schoolwork.

But although I tried to concentrate for more than an

hour I got very little done. I could not stop shivering, I seemed to get colder and colder.

After a bit I gave up and went downstairs for some tea, and even sitting huddled over the fire I could not get warm.

Mrs. Mariner touched my hand as I handed her my cup. "Harriet! You're frozen," she cried. "I think you must have caught a chill, maybe you'd better go to bed. Wait by the fire till I fill a couple of hot-water bottles and put them in for you," and she hurried into the kitchen.

I felt an awful fool but I really was thankful to snuggle down between the sheets, clasping my hot bottles fore and aft.

Mrs. Mariner peeped in to see if I was settled.

"I'm going up to collect my order from the shop," she said. "Look, swallow these and stay put till I get back." She put a couple of aspirins beside a glass of water on the bedside table and left me, and obediently I did as I was told.

Soon I began to feel drowsy and warm and I stopped shivering. I lay quiet and comfortable listening to the shrieking of the wind round the house, to the battering of the rain on the windows. The storm was more violent than ever and showed no signs of lessening. I was grateful to be safely indoors. How was it with Birney, I wondered? How much longer would he be able to hold out, to remain in hiding? Who else was hunting him as well as the police? What added danger might now threaten him from those in the village whose secrets he had discovered, whose symbol of power he had destroyed?

Chapter Fifteen

As it grew darker I lay listening to the ferocious wind, worrying about the awful mess Birney was in, and trying to find some way out of it.

I had never before in my life been really deeply involved with anyone, although I had friends, my relationships with them were casual. *This* with Birney was something quite different, with him I was involved up to the neck. I felt fiercely protective toward him and I knew he depended on me and trusted me—in fact I seemed to be the only person in the world he *did* trust, and this made me feel responsible for what became of him. He seemed to have reached a sort of crossroads, if only he took the right path now, he could find his way back again into a good way of living, he could make new friends, *real* friends who would help him to make a fresh start.

But in his present mood, only too easily he could make the wrong decision and sink deeper into trouble till he became a real criminal.

The choice depended on whether he could trust someone enough to accept the help they offered. I had tried my best to persuade him to get that help by giving himself up, but I had failed. Perhaps I didn't matter to him enough to influence his decision, yet he had destroyed the witch staff because it frightened me.

My life had been a sheltered one, my experience limited to my own kind of background. I had been brought up in a conventional way and had accepted without question the beliefs and values of my parents. I had never met anyone who had stepped outside the law like Birney, and I found the whole situation extraordinarily exciting, however frightening it might be. It was inconceivable that I should have become involved in such a different world from mine, yet here I was hiding a young criminal from the police, helping and protecting him, ready to fight for him, to cover up for him, and all because he had become so important to me, because I cared about him. Perhaps I *needed* somebody to care about, somebody within reach.

I slept uneasily, starting awake and dozing off only to be roused again by the rattling of the windows and the eerie moaning through the chinks and cracks which the wind can always find in an old house. I had a feeling that things were working up to some sort of climax, but there was little I could do about it.

When morning came, I felt wan and exhausted but recovered from my chill, and when Mrs. Mariner came in to have a look at me she easily persuaded me to stay in bed at least for breakfast, and ordered me to spend the day indoors and to keep warm. The storm had scarcely lessened, and the rain was as heavy as ever.

"I'm all right," I protested, thinking of Birney and wondering how I could manage to visit him. "Truly, I feel perfectly well again, it's just that the storm kept me awake in the night."

But Mrs. Mariner was firm. "No going out for you today, young woman," she said. So that was that and it was no use fretting and fuming. Birney would have to manage without me till the next day.

The postman brought a letter from our headmistress telling Mrs. Mariner that the repairs to the gas system were almost finished and since the coal strike was over, the school would reopen at the weekend—that left me only three more days at Mariners.

Nancy, who of course, would not be able to go back for some time, spent the day crowing over me. I wrote to my parents, finished a history essay and got up for lunch.

When Mr. Mariner came in, he was full of the policeman's visit to his quarries.

"Apparently they think that youngster who is missing may be in hiding somewhere around here. Bob Parkin would have searched my quarries I believe if it hadn't been so wet, but he'll be back, he said, when storm's blown out," said Mr. Mariner.

I grew cold with alarm, the cord was drawing tighter, the search growing closer.

"I think myself he'd be more likely in this weather to hide somewhere in a village," Mr. Mariner went on, "somewhere like Gramma Cobbley's—the cellars under her cottage haven't been opened since I was a boy, I bet."

"D'you mean Gramma would shelter him, help him?" I asked innocently. "Why?"

"Because she's a tough old character, a stubborn old cuss, and she doesn't like the law! Well, I'd better be getting back to work and try to keep my men going," he said stamping off. "This strike threat is very worrying."

I felt dreadfully upset by his news, the working quarries were getting too near the mark! If Bob Parkin really meant to search them, he might get the idea of looking next in the old quarries by the sea! And then what?

Meantime the storm raged on. When I went to bed that night the rain was still pelting down, as it had been for twenty-four hours, though the wind was coming in fierce gusts with lulls between, which might mean it was beginning to die down.

I was quite right, for when I woke in the morning the first thing I noticed was the quietness, the wonderful stillness and silence—the storm had blown itself out and was over at last.

I crept out of bed and opened my window, which I had wedged shut the night before because of the wind. Outside there was a thick sea mist, smothering everything in a mournful grayness.

I leaned out of the window trying in vain to distinguish the outline of the fruit trees in the garden, and then I heard them—from out of the muffling mist came the beat of innumerable invisible wings circling the house. I waited listening, tense with delight and in a moment they were all gone, out to sea. Once again the house had given them shelter, whoever they were, and I liked to think that they had kept us under their protection. I felt reassured, and my heart lifted a little in spite of my increasing anxiety about Birney.

Several times during the day that followed I found my mind going back to that early morning experience and gathering courage and hope from it. Events followed one another so quickly that it is difficult for me to remember clearly the exact timing, but I will try.

I was the first to arrive downstairs for breakfast so I got on with making the coffee and began to fry some eggs and bacon.

It was Wednesday and officially early closing at the village shop—closing of the *front* door anyway—and I remember thinking that I must get Birney's food during the morning. —Money! I was running out. I had better ask Mr. Mariner for some more, my father would make some arrangement to pay him back what he lent me, I knew.

I tackled him when he finished his bacon and eggs and had looked up from his letters for a moment to pass over his coffee cup for more.

"How much d'you need? Is it for something special?" he asked. "You've spent what you brought with you pretty quickly haven't you? You women are all alike."

I thought I had better have some to spare in case Birney needed it.

"I'd like to have £5 please," I said boldly.

"That's quite a lot of extra money!" Mr. Mariner exclaimed. "D'you really need that much? What will your father say?"

"He won't mind, and I do need it for something special," I pleaded.

"All right, I'll get it from my desk when I've finished my breakfast," he agreed, returning to his letters, which were claiming most of his attention.

Mrs. Mariner had not yet come downstairs or she might have wanted to know why I needed more money. What was there to buy in such a small village?

I went into the kitchen to make some fresh coffee and when I came back Mr. Mariner handed me the notes. "There you are," he said, "don't spend it too quickly."

I thanked him and put the notes into my pocket, and I felt a bit guilty.

"And, Harriet," he continued putting his arm round my shoulders, "I don't want to alarm you, but be a little careful, don't go too far away alone. If this boy really is hiding somewhere in our area, he may be violent, even dangerous—desperate more likely, poor chap—I wouldn't like you to get a fright."

"I'll be careful," I promised. "What will happen to him if they catch him?"

"He'll be sent back to his approved school I suppose."

"Would you help a boy like that if you found him?" I asked.

"I wouldn't help him to *escape*," said Mr. Mariner scratching his head and frowning thoughtfully. "I'd have to hand him over to the police, they're bound to catch him in the end. But after that I might help him to get onto his feet again if I could and give him a chance to go straight."

I nodded, it was just what I'd have expected him to say. Once Birney gave himself up, he could count on Mr. Mariner for help. But how was he to be persuaded to do that?

I had just finished filling a thermos of coffee for Birney when Mrs. Mariner appeared.

She looked a bit surprised and I went to refill the coffee jug for her.

I'm going out on the cliffs for a little," I explained. "I feel restless after staying indoors all yesterday. I thought I'd take a hot drink with me."

"A good idea," said Mrs. Mariner, "but should you be going out at all? The mist seems pretty thick, and you did have a chill, you know."

"I'm all right, really, and I won't go far," I promised. I put the thermos into my shoulder bag, pulled on my anorak and was out of the house before she had second thoughts. I couldn't wait even another minute to see if Birney was all right.

I blessed Mrs. Mariner's vagueness, her unsuspicious mind. If it had been Nancy, she'd have realized at once that something fishy was going on—no girl in her senses goes out for pleasure on a morning of thick mist with a thermos of coffee tucked under her arm—but apparently Mrs. M. had noticed nothing unusual—maybe she thought I was batty anyway.

I hurried down the path toward the cove, and when I looked back the house was completely blotted out. I had the strangest feeling of isolation, as if I were quite alone on the earth. The dense mist seeping up from the sea seemed to shut me off from the rest of humanity in a strange unreal world of utter silence. I couldn't hear a sound, not even the cry of a bird.

When I reached the rock shelf where the caves were, I had to go very cautiously, almost feeling my way. It was all rather scaring and suddenly I needed Birney, the warmth of his hand, his solid presence beside me. I began at once to whistle our tune—

> "Bobby Shafto's gone to sea,
> Silver buckles at his knee—"

there was no answering whistle. In this intense stillness how could he not have heard?

I repeated the tune to the end, bravely at first then falteringly as my alarm grew till finally I stopped. By this time I ought to have reached the entrance to the outer caves—but it was impossible to see them through the mist which blotted out the entire area.

Then I began to panic—what could have happened to him, he *must* have heard me! Forgetting all need for caution I began to shout at the top of my voice. "Birney! Birney! Birney!"

There was no answer.

Chapter Sixteen

I was really frightened by then and my imagination was working nineteen to the dozen—he had had a fall and broken his leg, he was lying unconscious, he had been picked up during the night by searching police, he had decided to take himself off without a word to me or anyone, or, worst of all, someone had dealt with him as they had with that other boy, after Candlemas. I tried to pull myself together. This was ridiculous, it was the twentieth century and such things did not happen—but I knew perfectly well that sometimes they *did*. I thought of Birney's face as he stood looking down on the ashes of the staff; he had looked scared as if he half-believed in reprisals. I thought of Gramma saying she'd have to pay for even *telling* me about the staff, surely it was all nonsense, my common sense told me—and yet . . . and yet.

Then I remembered my flashlight, and taking it out of my pocket I switched it on and turned it about. But its beam was too feeble to penetrate the mist, so I put it away again and began to feel my way over the boulders to where I was certain the entrance to the cave must be.

I put up my hand, trying to touch the stone of the roof—the cave must be here, it must!

At that moment an extraordinary thing happened, the mist suddenly thinned and lifted just enough for me to see where I was . . . to see the cave . . . *There was no cave.* I was in the right place, my back to the sea, and the gaping square-cut caves should have stood before me—there was nothing but a vast mass of tumbled rock and stone.

"Oh God!" I whispered, "the caves have fallen in!" Down came the mist again like an impenetrable curtain.

But I had seen enough to send me tearing along the path and up the hill to Mariners.

I threw open the door panting so that I could hardly speak.

"Help! quick get help!" I shouted. "The caves of the sea quarries—have fallen in—and there's a boy in there!"

Mrs. Mariner and Mrs. Pyke came running from the kitchen.

"What boy? When did you see him? How d'you know he's in there?" asked Mrs. Mariner.

"He's *living* there—camping—I've talked to him. Oh! don't waste time asking questions. He must be got out before it's too late." I was almost screaming at her in my desperation. I must have convinced her for without another word Mrs. Mariner picked up the phone and dialed for the police.

Nancy had staggered to the top of the stairs. "Better get on to Father," she shouted, "he can bring his quarry men to help. They'll have to clear all the debris before they can get him out. What a ghastly thing to happen!"

Mrs. Mariner succeeded in getting hold of Bob Parkin and told him briefly what had happened. "Harriet says there is a boy in there," she reported. "He must be cut off by the rockfall, so I doubt if he can possibly be alive."

She hung up and called upstairs, "Nancy, go back to bed at once." Then she rang Mr. Mariner to tell him.

I seemed to freeze up when I heard Mrs. Mariner say, "I doubt if he can possibly be alive." It was Birney they were talking about—Birney couldn't be, *mustn't* be dead!

Suddenly the room began to spin and my knees gave way—it was Mrs. Pyke who helped me into a chair and ducked my head between my knees.

"There," she said, "there, me dear, ye've had a nasty shock, no wonder yer upset. Are ye sure you seen a boy in the caves, yesterday was it?"

"Quite sure." I whispered. "*Absolutely* sure."

"Maybe he were only larkin' around like and went home to his bed afore anything happened," she suggested trying to comfort me. "Try not to worry too much. Bob Parkin will see to it, it's his job. Come into the kitchen now and I'll make you a cup o' tea."

I followed her into the kitchen, while Mrs. Mariner went up to get Nancy back into bed.

"I don't understand it," I said, "how could the caves fall in? It's unbelievable."

"Sometimes it happens after a storm in them old quarries," said Mrs. Pyke, "maybe the rain loosens the rock or somethin'. There were some fell in further along the coast after a storm a year or two back."

She handed me a cup of tea and I warmed my hands on it as I sipped its comforting sweetness.

Birney! What had happened to Birney? My mind churned round and round. Was he still in there, buried behind those tons of rock, safe perhaps but unable to get out? Or had he escaped from the police, from me, from life, forever? I couldn't bear to think of the awful things that might have happened to him, but it was impossible to think of anything else. The tea must have pulled me together, for I found I was able to think clearly again and the most urgent thought in my mind was that I must talk to someone, someone who would listen, but who?— Gramma of course! I must go to her at once and tell her the whole story. What an enormous relief it would be not to have to carry the burden of silence round with me anymore—and of course with Birney's life in danger there was no longer any question of keeping silent.

I knew there would be questions, endless questions from the police, from Mr. and Mrs. Mariner, perhaps even from the press, but I wasn't ready for them yet, my whole being was in a turmoil of anxiety over Birney's safety. I needed time to breathe, time to recover; I knew that Gramma would hide me till I felt able to cope again.

I slipped out quietly, no one saw me go, and I crept up the path through the mist. Soon I heard voices and feet coming down the hill, and I dived down a bank till they'd passed. It was Bob Parkin—I recognized his voice—and some of the men from the village making for the cove.

Mr. Mariner and his quarry men must be following by truck when they'd collected the necessary gear.

I took the shortcut across the fields, running so as to reach Gramma's cottage before anyone saw me. When I reached her door I gave one tap and burst in gasping for breath. "It's me, Gramma," I panted, "a terrible . . . thing has happened . . . the old sea quarries have . . . collapsed, fallen in . . . and my friend Birney . . . is buried behind them." My voice broke and I blinked back the tears that were stinging my eyes.

Gramma was sitting in her chair by the window, her cap askew, her head fallen slightly forward. She didn't answer me and I thought she was asleep.

I laid my hand on her shoulder and shook her gently, repeating what I'd said a bit louder.

She didn't waken, she didn't move but her head slipped farther forward and her mouth fell open. With a terrible realization I looked at her more closely.

Gramma was dead.

Her hand was not yet quite cold, and she looked quite normal. I just could not believe that she was gone—it was too much.

I knelt down beside her, trembling with shock and put my head on her knee, a paroxysm of grief shook me and I burst into tears.

I crouched there sobbing for goodness knows how long. I knew I must get up and go and tell someone, but I couldn't make my body move, it was too great an effort even to get up. I sank down onto the floor and stared at the old face. What had happened to her—heart failure? Had she died of shock, of fright? I remembered what she had said about reprisals when she told me about the staff. Surely such things were impossible . . . yet Gramma herself had believed in them. Anyway, she was gone, and no one would ever know now.

I got up off the floor at last and laid her hands together on her lap—her work was finished, her journey ended. I wandered round the room for a little, touching her things, her clock, her teapot, the bowl of early snowdrops on her windowsill, the family photos, her old balaclava hanging from a nail on the door. Then I stood for a long moment studying her face, I wanted to remember her and her cottage just as it was, to keep intact my picture of the gallant old woman.

When I looked out of the window, the mist was as dense as ever, but I knew I must not delay any longer.

I went over to the sink and washed my face in cold water, hoping to brace myself for whatever was to follow. First I had better go back to Mariners to tell Mrs. Pyke of Gramma's death, then perhaps on to the caves to face Bob Parkin's questions and to see how they were getting on with clearing a passage through the rockfall and rubble. I was terrified of what they would find once they got through, surely Birney couldn't possibly still be alive, but I dreaded to know for certain.

I had turned the handle of the door and was just about to leave when a faint sound near the sink stopped me.

I saw the bucket under it move slightly, tilt, then tip right over.

A square in the floor, a sort of trapdoor began slowly

to open . . . and out of it appeared the tousled head . . . of Birney. He looked scared to death and his face was filthy.

"Harriet!" he gasped and his voice came out in a sort of squeak. "Oh Harriet, it's wonderful—to be alive!"

He eased himself out of the hole, crawled across the floor and stood up. We threw our arms round each other and clung together.

"*Birney!* Are you really all right?" I asked, as anxiously my hands patted his shoulders, his arms, his head and his dirty face. "How on earth did you manage to get out, and unhurt too? Oh Birney, I was sure you were dead." Tears of relief began to run down my cheeks but I didn't care.

"I'm O.K." he said, "but it was a very near thing. I thought I was finished when the roof of the outer cave fell in and my way out was cut off. I just crouched there shivering for ages wondering what on earth to do. I've never been so frightened, so petrified, in all my life! Then when the dust cleared a little and the bits of stone seemed to have stopped falling, I struck a match. I had the idea of trying to find a way out through the back of the cave —there was something you once said about smugglers using a passage that came up into the village—well, I found it and here I am." I had never heard Birney make such a long speech before.

"And you're really all right?" I asked again, scarcely able to believe it.

"Yes," he said, "only terribly hungry. Where am I?"

"In Gramma Cobbley's cottage in the village," I said.

His glance fell on Gramma seated in her chair.

"D'you think she'd give me something to eat?" he whispered.

"I'll find you something," I said, "Gramma certainly would have but she can't anymore . . . she's dead."

Birney's face froze.

"Good God," he muttered, "what happened?"

"I don't know," I confessed. "When I got here to tell her about the rockfall and how you were trapped behind it . . . I found her like this."

"Have you told anyone about me?" he asked.

"Yes, I had to. Somebody had to try to get you out," I explained, "before it was too late. I told Mrs. Mariner and she rang the police. I'm sorry, Birney, but there was nothing else to do. I just said a boy. I didn't tell them who you are."

"So no one really knows who I am—then if I wanted to I could stay hidden—in the passage here under the cottage perhaps?"

"That won't be necessary," said a deep voice behind us. Framed in the doorway of the kitchen, solid and dependable, stood Mr. Mariner.

Chapter Seventeen

"Mr. Mariner . . ." I faltered, "how did you know . . . to come here?"

"I remembered my boyhood and the tunnel from the caves to Gramma Cobbley's cellar," he said. "Won't you introduce me to your friend, Harriet?"

"Oh . . . yes . . . sorry," I apologized coming to my senses suddenly, "this is Birney. Mr. Mariner, my friend's father, where I'm staying you know, I've told you about him."

Mr. Mariner strode across the floor, his hand out-stretched to Birney.

"You're lucky to be alive, son," he said. Birney hung back eyeing him for a minute as if he were sizing him up, then he stepped forward and shook hands.

"I know, sir," he said simply.

Then Mr. Mariner saw Gramma and tiptoed across the room to her, evidently thinking she had dozed off.

"She's not asleep . . . she's dead," I said.

"Poor old lady, heart failure I expect," said Mr. Mariner bending over her and nodding his head in confirmation. "Well, she had a long innings, and she was beginning to fail. When did it happen, Harriet? Were you with her? Have you told the doctor or anyone?"

"No, I had just discovered her when Birney turned up," I said.

"Well, run along to Mrs. Pyke's cottage and tell her, will you? She'll be home by now, and she'll get the doctor. And you, son," he said turning to Birney, "had better tell me your story. I'd like to help you if I can, and I'm sure that's what Harriet intends."

"Wait a minute, he's terribly hungry," I interrupted, "shall I find some food for him. I'll look in Gramma's cupboard."

Mr. Mariner nodded and led the way into the little-used front room, which Gramma called her parlor, while I collected a large plateful of almost everything I could lay hands on, and brought it in.

"Now," said Mr. Mariner in an authoritative tone to Birney, "sit down and get on with it." I shut the door and left Birney wolfing down the food, and Mr. Mariner digging out his story. Then I ran through the mist to Mrs. Pyke's cottage. Luckily she was home and came at once.

"It were the best way for 'er to go, poor wold soul, sudden-like, she never could a-bear to be ill," said Mrs. Pyke, "but she must a given ye a turn, finding 'er like that after what ye bin through already today, and that poor boy buried in the caves. Oh dear me, the pity of it! Bob Parkin says it'll take a tidy time to get him out if he's in there."

"He's not in there—he got out and he's all right," I cried joyously, "he's in Gramma's cottage now with Mr. Mariner."

"Well!" gasped Mrs. Pyke. "I do declare! I'm surely glad to hear it—that sounds like Bob Parkin now, headin' up this way. I do wish this wold mist would clear."

She was right, for in a minute the policeman appeared out of the mist, and when he saw me he said sternly, "I want a word with you, Miss."

"Gramma's gone," Mrs. Pyke told him, "slipped away with no fuss, I'm just goin' up to fetch the doctor."

"I'd better look in on the old lady," said the policeman, "and you come with me, Miss." I walked straight into the kitchen past the closed door of the front room and the policeman took off his cap and followed me.

"There she is," I said pointing to Gramma, "exactly as I found her—except that I laid her hands together."

"You take it pretty cool, I must say," the policeman said eyeing me rather reproachfully.

"Too much has happened today!" I exclaimed. "I can't feel anything anymore."

"Shocked I daresay," remarked Bob Parkin in a more

kindly tone. "Now just let me get my book out and you can tell me about it, if you please, and about the boy you saw in the caves—buried proper he must be by now." It was clear that the policeman did not altogether believe my story.

"The boy can speak for himself, Bob, he's here and very much alive."

Mr. Mariner came out of the front room with his hand on Birney's shoulder, and the astonished policeman wheeled on them, staring at Birney.

"Dang me, Corky Mariner, I never expected you to be here! And you're the boy?" he said to Birney, and I could see him putting two and two together in his mind. "Birnet Langdale is it?"

"That's right," said Birney calmly, "what are you going to do with me?"

Bob Parkin looked him up and down.

"You'll come along with me lad," he said grimly.

"But what are you going to *do* with him?" I burst out anxiously. "He won't run away again, will you Birney?"

Birney looked at Mr. Mariner and smiled slowly, and a look of understanding passed between them as if they had come to some sort of agreement. I felt enormously relieved at this and hopeful for Birney.

"No," he said. "I'm done with running away. Mr. Mariner has helped me to see that."

Bob Parkin looked at his watch.

"There'll be a police car in the village in half an hour or so on its routine call," he said, "they'll take you into the central station."

"Central station?—oh, you mean the police station in town?" I asked.

The policeman nodded. "Come along, lad," he said.

Birney turned to Mr. Mariner. "Good-bye, sir," he said, "you'll really do what you said?"

"Of course I will," Mr. Mariner laid a hand on his shoulder, "and you'll keep your side of the bargain?"

"Of course," said Birney with dignity.

Then he turned to me and held out his hands, and I took them in mine. I felt closer to him than ever before, now that he was leaving me. Was it the end? Would we ever meet again? He couldn't, mustn't disappear forever now.

I glanced at Mr. Mariner, then back at Birney's face and I had my answer. Mr. Mariner was not a man to let go.

"Harriet," Birney touched my cheek gently, shyly, "Harriet, thanks, for everything."

His voice sounded final somehow, and I had a moment of panic.

"But it's not good-bye," I said, "we'll meet again . . . won't we?"

"D'you really want to?" he asked.

"You *know* I do, and so do you," I replied.

"Then, we will," he said. He turned and walked off with Bob Parkin, his head held high, and as I watched, my eyes pricking with tears, I felt proud of him.

"I'll follow you to the station in about half an hour, Bob," said Mr. Mariner. "I want to have a talk with the chief and the social service department."

Then turning to me he took my arm. "Come along, Harriet," he said gently, "I'm going to take you home. You're worn out with all that's happened today, and no wonder."

He started to lead me toward the car but I hung back. "Just a moment," I said, "I want to say good-bye to Gramma before we go."

I went across to the window and lifted the bunch of snowdrops out of the bowl and placed them in Gramma's hands.

Just then Mrs. Pyke and the doctor came in, and I went out and got into the car beside Mr. Mariner.

The mist was thinning at last and looked as if it might soon lift.

"What will happen to him, to Birney?" I asked as we jolted down the track to Mariners. "He's not bad, really he isn't, though it was a dreadful thing he tried to do, he'll never do anything like that again. Will he be sent back to that horrible school? Will he be punished for running away?"

"He'll have to finish his sentence," said Mr. Mariner, "at the same school, he knows that. But the authorities are very fair, they'll see that he gets his chance to make a fresh start. I can offer him a job in the quarries to begin with when he gets his release. It'll be hard work, but he's a tough lad and keen to learn. Later on we can see how he shapes, he'll probably want to do something quite different. It's cars he's keen on, but this will give him a start."

"How did you persuade him to let you help him?" I asked.

Mr. Mariner smiled. "He didn't need much persuading," he said. "I think the fright he got when the caves fell in shocked him to his senses. He was more than ready to cooperate, thankful to be alive! Also," he went on with a twinkle, "I've no doubt you had something to do with his change of attitude."

I was pleased when he said that. "Where will he be living when he comes here?" I asked.

"We'll have to find him a foster home in the village, There'll be no difficulty about that. He'll be under the care of the local authority, of course, but they're usually very sympathetic and I will offer to sponsor him for the first year anyway."

"And his mother?" I asked, "will he be able to see her again? He loves her very much, you know."

"We'll have to leave that to the authorities too, and it will take time but I'm sure they'll arrange a meeting somehow if it's possible, when Birney is ready for it. I may be able to help there as well," said Mr. Mariner.

"Oh *thank* you, you are good," I cried, "he needs somebody like you, somebody he can trust."

"He needs you too, Harriet, somebody he can love. You're the one who has brought him round the corner, now together we must bring him inside again."

When we got to the house, Mrs. Mariner packed me straight off to bed with a hot-water bottle and a mug of soup, and she asked no questions.

I slept for hours, the deep dreamless sleep of utter exhaustion, and when I wakened it was dark but I could see the stars in a clear sky—the mist had lifted and was gone. I had a great sense of tranquillity, of happiness.

Supper was ready by the time Mr. Mariner got in from the police station in town, and Nancy was allowed to get up and come down for the meal in her dressing gown, to hear the whole story.

"So what happens now?" she asked when I had told my

part. "Harriet has done pretty well, I think, what about you, Father?"

"I think we've all done pretty well," said Mr. Mariner, "all those concerned with the boy, after all he is a young *offender*."

"Yes, but he's Birney, he's special," I broke in.

"That's where he's lucky, he knows that he's come to really matter to someone," said Mr. Mariner. "Anyway as I was saying I had a long talk at the police station, mostly on the telephone with the social service people, and Birney will be given his chance to make a fresh start. It may take a month or two to arrange things but I think it will be all right, and we can expect him to start work at the quarries later in the spring."

"Well done, Pop!" said Nancy.

"Will he be at Moorhill till he comes here?" I asked.

"I expect so, but I'm sure he'll write and tell us," said Mr. Mariner. "He won't want to lose touch with us now."

"I'm fed up with this old bug of mine!" Nancy exclaimed. "It has made me miss the only exciting thing that's happened here in my lifetime!"

"You wait," I whispered, "you only know half of it yet!"

When Nancy went back to bed, I followed her upstairs to my room to start packing my things ready to go back to school.

When it was done I opened my window wide, climbed into bed, and lay in the darkness, quiet and relaxed, thinking of Birney, of myself, of my friends at Mariners and in the village, of the interdependence of human beings, those inside and those outside, of the storm that was over and the crisis that was past, of the new beginning and the promise of spring . . . after Candlemas.

. . . .

It was early in April when I came back to Mariners to spend the Easter holidays there as Nancy's parents had invited me to do.

The valley round the house was warm with spring sunshine and echoed with the plaintive cries of the young lambs calling to their mothers. The waves lapped lazily in the cove below the caves; it was a peaceful scene and seemed entirely unrelated to the sinister happenings of my earlier visit.

At Mariners we were waiting for Birney's arrival. I had had several letters from him since the day we parted, and now at last he was being allowed to come to start work in the quarries, under Mr. Mariner's supervision.

"Where will he be staying?" I asked.

"Mrs. Pyke will have him as her lodger," Mrs. Mariner told me. "She has moved into Gramma's cottage, you know. Mrs. Pyke will be good to him, she's a kind motherly soul."

I wondered whether Birney would have changed, what his mood would be, withdrawn or friendly? Had he in those past weeks been able to adjust to the idea of living an ordinary normal life again? All these things and many more I wondered anxiously about as we waited. Nothing seemed certain except that this was a chance for a new beginning for him, and that I was overjoyed to be seeing him again.

There was a sumptuous tea ready on the table; we had

all helped to prepare it, for this was a celebration, a turning point in at least one life.

I saw him from the window coming striding down the path, his head high, his step eager.

"Here he comes!" I cried. We all moved to the door and Mr. Mariner threw it open.

Birney's face lit up and he quickened his pace to take Mr. Mariner's outstretched hand.

"Come inside," said Mr. Mariner.

"Thanks," said Birney, "I will."